THE
UNTAMED

USA *TODAY* BESTSELLING AUTHOR
K WEBSTER

CONTENT WARNING

Please be warned that this story contains incestuous relationships, voyeurism, sexual assault, and domestic violence of a side character, murder, and other scenes or themes that could be triggering to some readers. Read with caution.

I live in the Alaskan wild with my family because it's
where I belong.
Safe. Loved. Protected. Happy.

Beyond our home is a violent, ruled society I don't ever
care to encounter.
My oldest brother already went that route,
and it ruined him.
Being around strangers means heartache,
pain, and misery.
I'll stick with what I know because that doesn't hurt.

All I need are my siblings.
They're my best friends.
Life is fun with them.
Together, we're free in the wild.

But the wilderness is also the home of predators.
Bears, bad weather, sickness.
Other people.

We thought we could live alone and
unmolested by the latter.
We were so wrong.

With their sudden presence,
everything about our lives is challenged.
Loyalties become twisted.
Hearts get tangled in the chaos.
Feelings and urges cross impossible lines there's no
coming back from.
Bewildering. Depraved. Perverted. Dark. Vile.

My secret desires are wrong.
They threaten everything I hold so dear.
I could fight against it if I were alone in these
forbidden thoughts.

I'm not.
We're in this together.

Our love is untamed.
And we are the unruly.

The Untamed is a second generation forbidden romance in the Wild World taking place on the timeline after The Wild and The Free. While it's not necessary to have read the other two books, please note these characters are the children of Daddy Reed from The Wild. You'll see all of the characters from The Wild and The Free in The Untamed. Please read trigger warnings before proceeding.

63 REED
40 DEVON

22 ROWDY
19 RONAN
18 RYDER
17 RAEGAN
14 DESTINY
5 DAKOTA
3 DECLAN
1 DAWSON

The Jamison Family

REED   **DEVON**

ROWDY   **RONAN**   **RYDER**   **RAEGAN**

DESTINY   **DAKOTA**   **DECLAN**   **DAWSON**

WILD WORLD
BY K WEBSTER

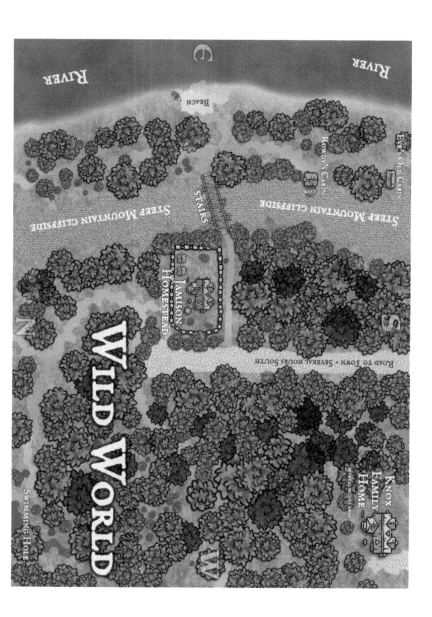

RIVER

RIVER

BEACH

ROWDY'S CABIN

CAVE

ELIE'S OLD CABIN

STEEP MOUNTAIN CLIFFSIDE

STAIRS

STEEP MOUNTAIN CLIFFSIDE

N

JAMISON HOMESTEAD

S

WILD WORLD

ROAD TO TOWN • SEVERAL HOURS SOUTH

KNOX FAMILY HOME

SWIMMING HOLE

W

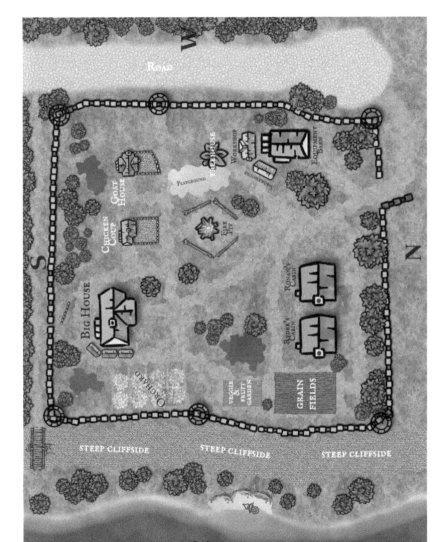

THE
UNTAMED

CHAPTER ONE

raegan

*R*UN FASTER.

He's going to catch you, Rae.

Tears burn my eyes from the chill of the early fall Alaskan air that also makes my breath come out in white-clouded puffs. My lungs ache and my calves are on fire.

I won't let him catch me.

I won't.

My determination to outrun him has another shot of adrenaline surging through my veins. New resolve to beat him has me darting off the pathway between the trees into the thicket. Branches lash out at me, seemingly accomplices on his side. A particularly sharp one snags at my hair. I strangle the cry of surprise in my throat, not eager to give away my new location.

Snap.

Too late.

"Raegan Abigail Jamison!"

He only calls me by my full name when he's pissed. This thought fuels me faster, ignoring the painful whip of icy wind and cruel branches, each taking their turns to punish me for him.

The snarled way in which he says my name feels closer. Too close. If Dad were here, he'd save me.

But he's not.

I'm all alone with no one to intervene.

I could stab him. The thought has me cackling, unable to suppress the crazed sounds slipping past my lips. It could be defeat that has me sabotaging myself and giving up my location.

He won't hurt me.

He can't.

Dad would whip him into next week.

Another bubble of laughter bursts out.

Snap. Snap. Snap.

Twigs break under his heavy boots right behind me. So close. There's nowhere to run. He's going to catch me. I grip the hilt of the too-big knife tighter than before. Even though it's cold, winter promising its annual return, my hands are slick from sweat inside my thick gloves.

"Got you!"

The words are hissed half a second before strong arms encircle my waist. I shriek in surprise, stumbling over my own feet, and go down hard, taking him with me. We hit the cold, unforgiving earth with a thud that probably scares off any game within a hundred-mile radius. Pain assaults me from every direction—elbows and knees quickly bruising, the sting of my lip that must've been pierced by a tooth, and every single muscle on fire from exertion.

"Get. Off. Me!" I bite out my words as I attempt to wriggle out from his massive frame. It's unfair, really, how he can have all the height and weight and muscles. I'm skin and bones beside him. I hate how strong he is despite our close ages.

"Give it back to me, Rae, so fucking help me."

His threats don't work on me. I've heard them a million times before. Though I may be smaller, I'm not afraid of him. I just hoped I'd be faster. Once again, I'm proved wrong.

He struggles to take the knife from my grip, but I manage to keep my hold on it. After seconds of not being able to take it from me, he takes another tactic, choosing to flip me over onto my back. His large hand easily covers my wrist, pinning it to the cold ground.

Ryder.

My brother.

Big, arrogant asshole.

I attempt to spit at him, but his other hand crushes my mouth, already keen on my underhanded tactics having been on the receiving end of them for as long as I can remember.

"Give me my knife back," Ryder growls, blue eyes burning bright with rage.

Since he won't let me spit—or speak—I glower at

him, my nostrils flaring. His body, tight with fury, is substantial against mine and we both breathe heavily from our jaunt through the woods.

It was my knife first.

If he'd let me speak, I'd remind him of that. This battle has been going on between us for two straight years. Ever since Uncle Atticus brought it to us. The hilt is made of elk bone and has stars carved into it. It was the most beautiful thing I'd ever seen. But, before I could claim it, Ryder snatched it up. He stole it from me.

To punish him for taking what was supposed to be mine, I spend a good portion of my days stealing it back. Some days, I win and have it in my possession before Ryder discovers it's missing. Other days, he catches me in the act and chases me down until he gets it back.

It's an infuriating game between us.

If he'd just hand it over for good, I'd leave him alone.

I mumble words that don't escape the confines of my mouth, hoping he'll relent on his hold on me. He narrows his eyes but eases up his hand that covers my lips.

No gloves.

His hand should feel like ice, but it's surprisingly warm. He'd been inside the big house, helping Mom with Declan, when I'd seen he'd left *my* knife on the kitchen table. Pouncing on the opportunity, without much thought, is what makes me a good hunter.

I just wish he weren't a better hunter.

I'm tempted to bite my brother's hand, but that'll

only anger him further. At this point, I have to accept defeat. Our eyes lock and his expression, contorted into one of fury and exasperation, softens slightly. When he's not fired up and pissed off, he typically wears an easy smile that lights up his blue eyes.

I lick his hand to see if his boyish grin will make an appearance, forgiving me long enough for him to release me.

He doesn't smile.

His body tenses and his lips tug into a frown. Something hardens between us. My eyes widen as crimson floods his cheeks.

"Fuck," he snarls, pushing away from me as though I'm diseased.

I sit up on my elbows, amused by the way his penis makes his jeans bulge. Just wait until I tell Ronan about this.

"You got hard," I say with a laugh. "What's wrong with your penis?"

He winces, turning his back to me. "Shut up, Rae."

"Why is it hard?" I demand, amused at his unusual behavior. "Is it broken?"

"I said be quiet!" His angrily spat out words echo in the forest.

"Does Dad know your penis is broken? Maybe he'll take you into town to a penis doctor!" I crack up laughing, enjoying the way he shudders in horror. "Is it contagious?"

"Stop being a bitch."

His words are a punch to the gut. Usually, he waits around to see my response whenever he says something mean, because he obviously enjoys taunting me. Not today. He storms through the thick brush away from me as though I'm the one carrying the broken penis disease.

"Come on, Ryder," I call after him. "I was kidding. Don't be a baby."

He doesn't respond. I sit up and turn the elk bone knife over in my hand. If he left his knife without any more fight, it means I won this battle. For some reason, I don't feel like it was a fair fight, though. Like my teasing words had more of an impact than I realized.

Maybe his penis is broken.

What if he really is sick?

My stomach tightens. Once, Mom got sick with pneumonia when she was pregnant with Destiny. I thought she was going to die. Where we live, there aren't any doctors. Luckily, both she and Destiny pulled through.

What if Ryder doesn't?

He may annoy me every day, all day, but the thought of losing him forever makes my blood run cold in my veins. A ball of emotion forms in my throat. It takes a lot to make me cry. I especially never cry when it comes to Ryder. So why do I feel like I might burst into tears any second.

Ugh.

Screw Ryder. He's probably fine and I'm worrying over nothing. Tomorrow he'll be back to bothering me like usual. In the meantime, I'll do what I always do when I need cheering up.

I'll go see Ronan.

The gate to our three-acre homestead stands wide open, which means Ryder's around here somewhere. I quickly scan our fenced-in land, pausing to admire our home. Everyone, over the years, has pitched in to make this place pretty spectacular.

Straight forward, the circular firepit is the focal point. Dad and Ryder spend a lot of time handcrafting the wood bench seating into two C shapes with the pit in the center. The details they put on the woodwork are intricate and impressive.

To the right, the massive equipment barn looms as the largest structure aside from the big house. Dad stores in it all the machinery he needs for building and keeping this place going. He also keeps the riding mower and extra gasoline there. The large garage bay is closed, which means no one's using any of the machines today.

In front of the equipment barn is a small smokehouse where Dad smokes any fish or game we kill. Beside that is his workshop where he welds or builds furniture. Out in front of the workshop is a play area for the kids, including a treehouse that me, Ronan, and Ryder hung out in a lot of time up until they got their own cabins. Dad spends a lot of time in the workshop as the little kids love playing on the swing set or in the treehouse while he works.

At the far-right corner, there's a goat house with a chicken coup to its left, both complete with their own pens, and a small man-made pond behind them. The ponds on our property have been here for as long as I remember. Uncle Atticus and Dad made them not long after they built the big house.

The big house runs from near the chickens all the way along the south fence to the orchard that sits on the west end of the homestead. Behind the house is a root cellar and kitchen greenhouse, the big playground for the kids, and several clotheslines where Mom can do laundry while keeping an eye on the littles.

Our orchard is one of the best places to disappear to when avoiding chores. You can sit under the shade of an apple tree and eat your belly full until you're bursting.

On the northeast corner is the food jungle. Really, it's just two large sections of grains with several thinner rows of small fruits and another section for all the vegetables. There are small ponds near both the orchard and the food jungle that allow us to easily water the vegetation.

And finally, to my left, on the north side between the food jungle and the gate, are the two neighboring cabins that belong to Ryder and Ronan.

It really is beautiful here.

I should probably go to Ryder and maybe apologize

for giving him a hard time, but I don't exactly want to. He's probably sitting in his hammock in his little house, playing his guitar, and sulking. As much as I love hearing him strum and make music, I'd rather see Ronan.

Ronan's my best friend in the whole world.

I set off on the path toward the twin cabins. All three of my older brothers have their own homes. It's not fair. Dad says it's because when a man turns eighteen, they should have their own home so they can start making a life of their own. Rowdy lives in the old cabin by the river. When Ronan and Ryder each turned sixteen, we all pitched in to help build them their own places.

Sixteen and seventeen came and went for me.

Still no home.

Heck, I can't even go up on the roof alone to have three seconds of peace without the whole family losing their minds with worry. I'm fragile and something that always needs protecting according to them.

All thoughts of our property and its beauty turn dark.

It's so unfair. It's probably because I'm a girl and my parents think I need extra protecting. My mood sours considerably by the time I reach Ronan's porch. Since both his and Ryder's houses are next to the food jungle and on the north side of our property, it allows them the privacy I don't have being that I share a room with my fourteen-year-old sister Destiny at the big house.

I start to knock on Ronan's door but remember I

don't have to. Only Ryder demands we knock before entering. God, he's so weird. The front door creaks open
and my gaze sweeps over the small space. His room
smells like peaches and cinnamon. My stomach growls
for a snack, though dinner will be ready at dusk, which
will be soon.

"Hey," I grumble in greeting, pushing the door
closed behind me.

Ronan lifts his gaze from the book he's reading. I'm
immediately warmed by his welcoming, brown-eyed
stare. His glasses are slightly askew and I can't help but
grin back at him.

"Uh-oh," he says, setting the book on the end table
and patting the bed beside him. "What'd he do now?"

The fact Ronan knows me like no one else does fills
me with pleasure. I untie my boots, pull them off, and
then pad across his wood floors to his bed. He studies
me as I climb into bed next to him.

This is where I want to be.

Not sharing a room with Destiny, but sharing one
with my best friend. My favorite sibling. My Ronan.

"Can I come live with you?" I blurt out.

His eyebrows furl together and a frown tugs at his
full lips. "Mom said no, remember?"

I roll my eyes, irritated at the reminder of that argument. It was only last month that I told Mom I was
going to live with Ronan. She flipped out and yelled at
me. We both ended up crying by the end of the fight.
Dad diffused the situation, but the answer was still no.

No reason as to why not.

Just no.

Again, so unfair that my brothers can do what they want, but I have to follow Mom and Dad's dumb rules.

"I hate everyone," I tell him with a huff. "You're the only one who gets me."

"You don't hate everyone."

I ignore his comment because I do hate them. He smiles as I reach up to brush away a dark blond-ish-brown lock of hair that falls into his eyes. His hair is always messy and overgrown. I love the way it looks on him. Just like I love his silly black-rimmed glasses. I've put them on a million times since he got them a couple of years ago and still don't understand how he can see through the blurry glass.

"Are you going to tell me what happened?" Ronan takes hold of my hand that's fussing with his hair and squeezes it.

My heartrate quickens. He's the best cuddler. "Ryder."

He smirks, patting the sheath on my belt at my hip. "You still have your knife."

"He was acting weird and gave up."

"Our brother gave up?" Ronan chuckles. "That doesn't sound like him at all."

I note that Ronan hasn't moved his hand from my hip. My skin tingles where he touches me. A shiver runs through my entire body.

"He got hard." I narrow my eyes as I study Ronan, waiting for a reaction.

"Hard?"

"His penis, Ro. He pinned me down and it got hard."

His face pales and an unfamiliar chill chases away all the warm, fuzzy feelings he evoked.

"What?" I demand, my heart rate thumping wildly in my chest. "Is he sick?"

Ronan flops onto his back and stares up at the ceiling. "I don't know."

"You're not telling me something."

The room falls into silence again.

What are they hiding from me?

CHAPTER TWO

ronan

H E GOT HARD.

She said it so breezily. As if it meant nothing. As though the words were just words and not a strike into the earth of my world, sending fissures scattering in a thousand different directions.

He. Got. Hard.

I'm both sickened and oddly intrigued all at once.

"Should I tell Mom and Dad?"

I jolt upright, shaking my head at her. "No. Don't say anything."

Raegan's eyes narrow to tiny slits. She reminds me of a hawk when she's trying to get to the bottom of something, attention hyper focused and ready to swoop in on her prey. "Why not? If he's sick, they should know."

A groan of frustration echoes through me. Dad gave me and my brothers "the talk" when we were old enough to start getting spontaneous erections. He even explained how it was okay to relieve yourself in the shower or when you're alone—that, one day, when you have a wife, it's how you'll impregnate her.

I don't want a wife and I certainly don't want to impregnate her.

"It just happens sometimes to guys," I say vaguely. "The same sort of stuff happens to girls probably."

"We don't have penises," Raegan states, a dark brow arching high. "Our nipples get hard when we're cold, but yours do too." She pinches one of my nipples through my shirt, making me cry out in surprise. "Why does it just happen? I don't understand."

Dad said, under no circumstances ever, were we to talk to our sisters about sexual intercourse or the anatomy of our bodies. Mom was in charge of explaining things to the girls.

"I'm not allowed to tell you," I admit in defeat.

Raegan blinks hard several times as emotions take turns flickering over her face. First, there's fury. Her brown eyes flame hot with her anger. Then, it switches to confusion before landing on hurt. Her pouty lips tug into a frown and I feel like a dick for doing this to her.

We tell each other everything.

Well, *almost* everything.

Some secrets are better left unsaid or even never thought of. I keep those under a tight lid.

"You're all assholes," Raegan hisses. "Maybe I should run away. Go live with Aunt Eve and Uncle Atticus."

It's an empty threat. She hates Wild, their oldest son.

"You're not leaving me here." I take her hand, tugging her to me. "You belong here."

The tension bleeds from her body as she cuddles into my side. I nuzzle my nose into her hair that smells of leaves and pine. I love how my sister always reminds me of the earth, like she's born from the dirt and not Mom's womb.

"Tell me why his penis got hard." She pauses and then huffs. "I won't tell Dad you told me."

I let out a sigh of resignation. "Guys just sometimes get an erection. A penis is, uh, extremely sensitive."

"Is yours sensitive?"

Heat warms my cheeks. I'm not exactly thrilled about discussing this subject with Raegan, but she'll kill me if I don't give her some sort of answers.

"Yeah."

"Does it hurt?"

"Um, no. It feels good."

She grows quiet for a moment before speaking. "All Mom told me was a husband's penis goes in a wife's vagina and that's how women get pregnant."

Dad told us a lot more than that. He explained that when we find wives one day, we'll enjoy sex. That instead of relieving ourselves in the shower with our hands, we'd do it inside our wives. The cum is what makes babies. As much as I try to envision this elusive future wife with my cock inside her, I can't. I certainly can't explain all that to Raegan.

"Pretty much," I agree. "It needs to be hard to do that."

"Ryder's penis got hard." She pauses again. "He's my brother, not my husband, so it was because he accidentally rubbed it against me?"

I let out a rush of air. "Exactly. It was just an accident."

"That's why he was embarrassed."

"And that's why you can't tell Mom or Dad. They'll punish him. You know how weird they are about stuff like that."

She nods, frowning. Once, me and Raegan went swimming together in the river. We thought it'd be funny to take off all our clothes. I think we were like eleven and thirteen at the time. Dad tore my ass up with a belt and Raegan was grounded for a whole month. If they knew Ryder got an erection with Raegan, I feel like they'd probably react similarly.

"I won't tell," Raegan vows. "Has yours ever gotten hard with me?" She looks up at me from beneath her dark lashes, pink tinting her slightly freckled cheeks.

"No," I say forcefully.

Not with *her*.

Raegan flinches at my harsh reply and looks away. "Do you think that's why Mom doesn't want me to live with you? Because they think your penis is going to get hard and make me wind up pregnant?"

The thought is repugnant.

"Maybe, but you don't have to worry. I'm not going

to get you pregnant." I suppress a shudder. "I want to puke just thinking about you making my cock hard enough to ejaculate. Besides, you'll have Wild for that."

Now it's her turn to be disgusted.

"Wild is an arrogant twat," she grumbles. "'*I play football. I'm so great.*'" The way her voice deepens as she mocks Wild has me laughing. "'*I have a girlfriend. I have five girlfriends. I have a truck. I have a phone. Blah, blah, blah, I'm so amazing.*'"

I used to be envious of Wild and his life near town. He goes to a real school, not taught by his parents like we are, and is exposed to lots and lots of people. Rowdy was so intrigued, he went to live with Uncle Atticus and Aunt Eve for a few months several years ago. But, whatever happened, he didn't like it. Rowdy came back different. Quiet, sullen, reserved…and angry.

"Wild doesn't have five girlfriends. He's saving himself to marry you," I tease. "You'll have ten of his kids and then you'll be so amazing just like him."

She sticks her finger in her mouth and pretends to gag. "Gross. I'm not going to marry him. I'll marry you before I marry Wild. Dad would kill us both and that would still be better than having Wild's *amazing* ten-baby-making penis anywhere near me."

Wild is seventeen like Raegan. I feel like our parents are pushing that relationship whenever we see the Knox family, but Raegan's not biting.

"Will you ever leave home?" My voice grows somber. "Go to town or someplace else in the world?"

"Never. Not as long as you're here. Why? Are you planning on leaving?"

I'd be lying if I said I never thought about it. In fact, I wonder sometimes if I could be free to be myself outside of the wilderness we call home. But then I remember my one and only trip to town. Dad took me to get my eyes checked by a doctor who doesn't ask questions about where someone lives. I'd ended up needing glasses and subsequently got them after a couple days stay with Uncle Atticus and Aunt Eve. Dad took me to a movie and a couple of stores. I'd been overwhelmed to the point I thought I was going to suffocate. Later, I read up on it.

Panic attack.

I'd suffered a panic attack.

"You know I'll never leave this place. Or you." I lean over and kiss Raegan on the forehead. "Are you better now?"

She nods and smiles. "You make everything better, Ro. You always do."

When Raegan leaves to help Mom with cooking dinner, I can't help but pace my small cabin. My mind is spinning as I wonder how Ryder is feeling after the accidental hard-on. Is he humiliated? It's not something I can exactly ask. Not without some sort of awkwardness. If it were me that it happened to, I'd be mortified.

But it has happened to you…

Only difference is, I didn't get caught like Ryder did. It came and went without detection. Well, I had to *make* it go away by jerking off almost violently the second I was alone after the incident, but at least I didn't have any witnesses.

As if on cue, my dick thickens. Dinner will be ready soon, which means I don't have time to jerk off. But the more I try to ignore it, the more of a distraction it becomes.

I can do this quickly.

Sure beats risking an erection at the dinner table for all to see.

I've made my decision. I'll jerk off. My heart races in my chest as I open the bedside table drawer. The bottle of lube sits half-empty. I've gone through quite a few bottles in the past year, ever since Wild smuggled me some dirty magazines. Dad makes Uncle Atticus bring us lube from town and supplies us with it. It's awkward and embarrassing, but Dad says no one wants a raw dick, so he's looking out for us.

I switch off thoughts of Wild and Dad so I can focus on the magazines. They're all mostly of women with their legs spread and breasts on display. It's arousing to look at and helps me visualize this supposed wife I'll have one day. My favorite picture is in one of the magazines where all you can see is ass covering most of the page. Her fingers dig into her fleshy cheeks as she spreads herself apart. I'm always so fucking turned on by her tight, puckered pink asshole.

My cock jolts, begging for attention. With jerky movements, I unbutton my jeans before shoving them and my boxers down my thighs. I slather my cock with lube and then stroke the sensitive flesh.

Fuck.

Feels so good.

My eyes flutter closed as I attempt to visualize being inside a woman. It's hard to imagine. I sneak a peek at the magazine that's left open on my favorite page on the bed. Staring at her sexy hole, I begin relentlessly fucking my fist. I think about slicking up her hole and pushing inside her there. From what Wild says, the ass is supposed to be tighter than the pussy. He's had sex multiple times, if we're to believe his boasting, and tried many different positions, including anal.

Somehow my thoughts drift to Wild. His sculpted shoulders and cruel smiles. I'd never in a thousand years admit to my friend how many times I've jerked off thinking about him naked. I'm pretty sure Dad would send me upriver without a boat and rocks tied to my ankles if he thought I fantasized about being with a man sometimes.

My cock loses some of its stiffness as it should. Thinking of Wild isn't supposed to arouse me. I'm supposed to think up images of my future wife. I imagine she'll look like the girl in the magazine with her silky brown hair and bright blue eyes. I stiffen again, keeping my focus on her glistening pink hole.

A quiver of anticipation flutters through me as my nuts draw up. I'm going to come soon. Then all the rampant thoughts inside my head will quiet. I start stroking my cock faster and faster, eyes drooping closed as pleasure consumes me.

And then it happens.

The most forbidden image of them all enters my mind—one I try desperately to keep contained.

Ryder.

Shirtless, stretched out in his hammock, with his guitar in his lap. Dark hair in disarray. Long lashes fanning out over his tanned cheeks and a boyish grin teasing his full lips. Instead of the girl on the magazine's ass, I imagine my dick poised at Ryder's luscious lips.

Oh, fuck.

I come with a guttural growl. Cum shoots out of me with such force it splatters the magazine, soaking my favorite page. I'm lost in the fantasy, still locked in the way I imagine his mouth would look like painted with my cum.

So. Fucking. Beautiful.

As soon as I come down from my delightful high of allowing myself a brief taste of a forbidden fantasy, reality settles around me like a dense fog.

That was wrong on so many levels.

So. Wrong.

I'm supposed to find a wife. And not just any

woman, because if any woman would do, I'd choose Raegan because she's my best friend. She's my sister, so that can't happen.

So, when I think of Ryder this way, it's the worst of the worst.

He's a man and he's my brother.

No and no.

Bitterness creeps up my throat, sour and disgusting. Sometimes I hate this body and brain I was born into. It doesn't seem to want to follow the rules. I love my siblings and parents. Never would I do anything to hurt their feelings or make them feel like I was some sort of freak.

Which is why I'll take my secret to my grave.

CHAPTER THREE

raegan

MY HOUSE IS LOUD.

There's always a baby crying or a kid hollering. It's why I love escaping it. Ronan's house is the best. My favorite time is when just he and I are lying on his bed, both lost in our books, quietly escaping our world for another we know very little about.

"Raegan!"

Mom's voice cuts through my daydream and drags me to the present. She's rushing about the kitchen, grabbing last-minute items for dinner. I'm supposed to be helping, as dinner prep is one of my chores, but I'm doing a terrible job today.

Sometimes I'm jealous of Mom. Not because she has to deal with all these damn kids. No, I'm envious of her beauty. Her blond hair hits her about mid-back and she rarely pulls it into a ponytail like I do. Dad loves stroking his calloused fingers through the silky strands, which is probably why she leaves it down. Mom has a youthful appearance making her seem as young as me sometimes. Like we could be sisters. Maybe that's why we butt heads so often.

Nothing makes her smile like Dad does. The smile she saves just for him is radiant. As though he's the most handsome man on earth and she's lucky to have him. Everything about her seems to glimmer whenever he's in the room.

And Dad?

He stares at her like he wants to eat her alive. There's always a ravenous, feral glint in his eyes whenever she's near. I don't quite get it. I mean, she has stretchmarks from being pregnant a million times, so I don't understand what he finds so fascinating about her body. Even her boobs and butt are smaller than mine.

He must just be a sucker for a pretty face.

"Take these to the table," Mom says, thrusting a stack of plates at me, making a face that's anything but pretty. "Enough dillydallying."

I take the plates from her and manage to keep the eye rolling at bay until I've turned my back on her. All of my younger siblings are already at the table. I try to imagine a life one day where I'll be married with kids of my own.

I can't.

All I want to imagine is having my own quiet cabin or sharing one with Ronan.

"Da," Dawson cries out, smacking the surface of his highchair table. "Dadadada."

A jar of pureed sweet potatoes sits just out of reach with the spoon sticking out. I would feed him, but he only likes it when Dad does. No one else does it with sound effects and goofy faces, so he pitches a fit. There's enough chaos without the baby screaming too.

"Where's Dad?" I ask the other kids.

"Daddy had to wash up," Destiny says, cocking her head in my direction. "He smelled like animal guts."

Destiny, like Ronan, can't see well. But where Ronan's vision was corrected with glasses, Dez's is un-fixable. That's what the doctor told my parents when they took her into town. She's mostly blind and can only see dark shapes. Though she's fourteen and it's all she's ever known, I still think it must really suck for her. I can't imagine not being able to hunt or read.

Mom breezes out of the kitchen with a platter in hand. She sets it on the table before rushing back to the kitchen. Declan, only three, attempts to reach for one of the slivers of meat, but Dakota smacks his hand. At five, Dakota thinks he's Declan's boss.

"Kota," I chide, shooting Dakota a death glare. "Hit him again and I'll tear you up with Dad's belt."

Declan's lip wobbles and Dakota scowls at me. Mom is so busy with the baby and cooking, she lets Dakota get away with murder. Sometimes I feel like I'm Dakota's mom. If I really were his mom, I'd take great pleasure in spanking him for being such a brat.

"You can't spank me," Kota taunts as he pushes his

messy brown hair out of his eyes. "Daddy will spank you back."

I shrug and flash him an unbothered grin. "It'll be worth it. I bet I can spank harder than Dad."

"Da!" Dawson cries out, throwing both hands in the air. "Da!"

Heavy footsteps thud through the house, which means Dad's here. I shoot Dakota a warning look not to tattle on me or I'll tattle right back. Since there's nothing new about this relationship between me and my little brother, he wisely keeps his mouth shut.

Dad stops to kiss the top of each of our heads. I adore my dad. Where Mom is kind of bossy and annoying, Dad is fun and loving. He teaches us all the cool stuff like hunting and fishing and building cabins. All Mom wants me to do is be trapped inside this house like her, cooking and washing and cleaning. It's much more exciting hanging with Dad and my older brothers.

My dad is much older than Mom. I don't think I've ever asked what their age difference is, nor have I really cared. All I know is his messy, dark brown hair is streaked with lots of silver and his beard is also graying. Aside from the crow's feet near his eyes and the permanent scowl lines between his brows, he's otherwise a nice, fit specimen despite his older age and I can see why Mom practically melts in his presence. Dad is muscular, tall, and incredibly strong. He has this powerful, authoritative aura that draws you to him and implores you to be obedient.

Dad ruffles Dawson's hair as he comes into the dining area before sauntering over to Mom in the adjacent kitchen. She stops fussing over the stove to let him sweep her into his powerful arms. When I see them like this, I'm almost eager for my own future and husband. It gives me butterflies in my stomach. The way he holds her as though she's the most precious thing in his world and kisses her like she might vanish in an instant.

Would Wild be that way to me?

I nearly gag at the thought. Wild loves himself too much to love anyone else. I want someone like Dad.

Like Ronan.

Heat burns at my cheeks and I force my gaze elsewhere. The kids are chattering noisily, and I wish my older brothers were here. As if on cue, I see three tall, broad men through the window, walking along the gravel path from the gate to the big house.

Rowdy with his crazy man-bun and beard.

Ryder, who keeps playfully trying to jump onto Ronan's back.

And Ronan.

Beautiful, wonderful Ronan.

I stare at them until they disappear from sight on the porch. My heart trips over itself at the sound of thunderous footsteps entering the house behind me. Ryder is the loudest, greeting everyone as he enters. Ronan's hellos are more subdued, but at least he speaks. Rowdy doesn't say a word. I'm thrilled when Ronan chooses the seat beside me. Sometimes Ryder takes it to annoy me, but not today. He avoids eye contact with me at all costs. Even though that means I get what I want—Ronan, my knife, and Ryder to leave me alone—something niggles at me.

Something doesn't feel right.

Dinner is crazy like usual. Everyone talks over one another, trying to be heard. Our family is huge and if you want to say your piece, you have to have the loudest voice. Every now and again, Dad's voice will boom with his loving authority and it all calms back down.

"Can we go hunting tomorrow, Dad?" I ask when there's a lull in the usual dinner commotion.

Mom opens her mouth, no doubt to deny me, when Dad speaks up first. "Sure, sunshine."

"Your chores around here are beginning to slack," Mom says, frowning. "There's too much to do around here. Dad and the boys can handle it."

Kota sticks his tongue out at me, triumphant at my being denied. I glower at him and mouth the words, "Dad's belt" before turning to my parents to plead my case.

"It's not fair," I grumble. "Just because I have a vagina I have to clean and cook. It's stupid."

"Raegan," Dad warns, voice sharp like a blade.

I'm his little girl until it involves arguing with Mom. He protects her always, even from my words.

"I can do them," Ronan offers from beside me. "Rae loves hunting a lot more than I do."

I could kiss him for having my back. I'm not sure

that'd go over well with my parents, though, so instead, I reach over and take his hand, squeezing.

"That's why you're my favorite brother," I say with a grin meant only for him.

Ryder's glare burns into me and I shoot him a confused look. Is he still mad his penis got hard? I meet his stare with a vicious one of my own. Rather than grow angrier, his cheeks redden and he drops his gaze to his plate.

"The wilderness isn't safe for a girl," Mom says, finality in her tone. "You know, Reed, how I feel about that."

Dad's lips thin out and something sinister flashes in his eyes. He glances my way and then shakes his head. "Your mother is right."

"What?" I shriek. "That's not fair! I can use the shotgun better than Rowdy or Ryder!"

Ronan squeezes my hand, offering his support, but it doesn't help. Not when my family chooses to cage me all the time. It's maddening. When my parents treat me like I'm made of glass, it's times like this I crave a life outside of this one. Even marrying stupid Wild seems better.

I could be free.

Hot tears burn my eyes and my chin wobbles. I hate when I get so angry I cry. Defeated, I stare down at my blurred by tears fork on my plate, blinking until it sharpens into focus.

"I can protect her," Ryder says. "And she has my knife."

My head jerks up and I meet Ryder's bright blue eyes. "It's *my* knife and I can protect myself."

He smirks and my stomach twists happily. "Whatever you say, Rae."

Dawson hollers from his highchair, no longer interested in his baby food. Dad pulls him from his seat and into his arms. The baby tugs at his beard and slobbers all over him as he tries to kiss him. When I witness moments like this one, it makes my heart burn in an unfamiliar way.

Maybe I would like kids one day.

I'd prefer a husband over kids, though, if I had a choice.

"If Dad and Ryder are with her, she will be safe," Ronan rushes out, voice steady with conviction that makes my heart trip over itself with gratitude. "I can stay here in case Mom needs me."

Mom frowns at Ronan's words but doesn't argue. Dad studies Ronan for a minute before giving a clipped nod.

I release a harsh breath and break into a wide grin. A whole day of exploring the woods, tracking game, and shooting anything that moves is a thousand times better than dealing with crying kids.

The conversation moves on to Uncle Atticus and Aunt Eve coming to visit soon. I'm still smiling when I feel eyes on me. Ryder is gaping at me.

Do I have something on my face?

I scowl at him and swipe the cloth over my mouth.

Nothing. Why is he looking at me like something's wrong with me?

"What?" I mouth, heat prickling over my flesh.

His eyes drop to my lips and he shakes his head. I wait for an answer but get nothing. He clears his throat and then starts talking to Rowdy like nothing ever happened.

Something did happen, though.

Tomorrow, while hunting, I'm going to get it out of him.

I'll stab him with my knife if I have to.

I wake to moans.

It's not the first time I've heard the sounds coming from my parents' bedroom, but it's the first time I listened curiously.

Destiny breathes softly, deep in sleep, in her bed beside mine. Normally, when I hear the sounds my parents make, I ignore them and go back to bed.

Tonight is different.

I want answers.

Slowly, I creep out of bed so as not to wake my little sister. The wood floors are cold on my bare feet. I sneak out of the house sometimes late at night just to have a moment of quiet to myself. There's an eastern lookout in our yard that faces the river. I like to climb and just sit, enjoying the chirping of crickets, the rushing of the river from beyond the cliff our house sits on, and the rustling of the leaves as the wind sweeps by. Because of these trips alone, I've learned to creep around almost silently.

I slip out of my bedroom and make my way down the hall. Mom's moans are louder as I approach. Their door is closed but not locked. It's never locked because one of the little kids is always having a bad dream and crawling into their bed. Twisting the knob, I hold my breath to see if they've noticed the sound.

When I realize it's safe, I gently push open the door. I peek my head inside, searching the darkness for them. If Mom won't go into specifics of what goes on between a man and a woman, I'll find out myself.

Mom lies on the bed with the moonlight illuminating her naked body. Dad, also naked, has his face buried between her legs. Wet, slurping sounds indicate he's licking or sucking or kissing her there. On her vagina.

A flurry of butterflies flaps around in my stomach.

"Your pussy tastes so fucking good, Pip."

Pussy.

The guttural way with which he says those words has heat flooding to my own vagina—er, pussy. I shift on my feet, rubbing my thighs together.

"Reed," Mom rasps. "I can't take any more. Fuck me already."

"I want you to come all over my face," Dad commands as he reaches up to grope one of her small boobs.

"And then I'll split you wide open with my fat cock, baby. Promise."

Their words are filthy but send exhilarating shots of desire coursing through me. I try to imagine me and Ronan in that bed. Ronan's lips on my pussy. Ronan's commanding words promising what sounds like pain with his hard *cock*.

"So fucking wet," Dad croons. "You're so goddamn needy."

Mom whimpers and then cries out. Her body arches up off the bed as she trembles. I'm mesmerized by the way her pleasure seems to consume every fiber of her being.

"Good girl," Dad praises. "My good, sweet girl."

He crawls over her body, hiding her from my sight. All I can see are the sculpted curves of his back muscles and his firm ass. He reaches between them in the shadows and then his hips thrust hard. Mom's resounding moan leads me to believe he's put his penis—er, *cock*—inside her.

My *pussy* throbs.

As though it craves attention too.

I want to make myself moan like she does. As Dad continues to thrust inside of her, I let my fingers dance along my belly over my nightgown to my *pussy*. I seek out the throbbing part of myself, rubbing it with the tip of my finger.

Oh, God.

That feels good. Really good.

I bite down on my bottom lip to keep from making sounds that would reveal my lurking. I watch as Dad forcefully pushes Mom's thigh up and starts grinding slowly against her. It's dirty, but I time my own motions with my finger to the way he moves.

My skin prickles and heats as my knees weaken.

I feel like something wonderful is close.

All I need to do is keep rubbing.

Unable to keep going at their pace, I massage the throbbing spot faster and faster. Touching myself over my clothes doesn't seem good enough. I want to feel the bare skin. With a silent gasp of air, I push past the material, sliding my finger along the slit. My vagina is slick—from sweat or something I don't know. Though I'm curious to see why or discover the source, I ignore it for the time being, seeking out the good place again. My fingertip is wet now, so when I touch it, it's the most exquisite sensation I've ever known.

I rub in frantic circles, no longer interested in what my parents are doing, but instead finding what happens when I plummet over the edge that's near.

Closer. Closer. Closer.

God, so close.

I try to think of Ronan's mouth on me, but my distracted mind keeps flitting back to Ryder on top of me, his cock hard.

What if his cock was naked and wet, rubbing against me here?

The image is not the one I want to think about, but

it's there, and it makes my body sing. I'm about to leap off the edge when the baby starts to cry. Dawson, who still sleeps in their room, in a crib in the corner, fusses.

Seriously?

Dad makes a sound like he's found his own pleasure and then chuckles. Mom joins in, softly giggling. Why are they laughing? I'm on the verge of something great and the baby messed it all up.

Flustered, I give up and abandon the throbbing between my thighs. Anger swells up inside me, chasing away all the lingering pleasure.

Dad's footsteps thud over to Dawson and he can be heard whispering sweet things to the baby. Irritated, I creep back to my bedroom and fall back into bed, unsatisfied.

Why wouldn't Mom tell me about all that stuff? Maybe, if she did, I'd actually want to find a husband and get married. I'd probably try to make babies all day every day if I knew it felt that good.

If she hasn't told me of all the pleasure involved, what else hasn't she told me?

I guess if I want to know something, I'm just going to have to figure it out myself.

CHAPTER FOUR

ryder

STOP LOOKING AT HER ASS, DIPSHIT.

I can't.

Raegan's dark jeans really fit her lately. It's as though she painted them on her body. The swell of her ass is magical, slightly jiggling with each step she takes. I want to sink my teeth into one of her fleshy cheeks, leaving my mark.

Man, just look away and focus.

Dad holds up a fist, drawing my attention to him, and indicates for us to stop. I pause, listening for sounds in the forest, using every power within me to keep my eyes on the trees and not my sister's ass.

I hear it.

Rustling.

Raegan's ponytail swooshes from side to side as she tracks the sound. Her head is turned, giving me a view of her profile. I'm nearly as mesmerized by her lips as I am by her ass. God, I'm so fucked in the head.

My feelings for my sister are getting out of control. I'm not sure when she transformed from annoying little sister to…this. But it happened. One day she was driving me crazy and quite literally the next, my dick was getting hard every time I saw her.

Yesterday was awful.

My shameful secret was exposed. She felt my erection. How could I have been so careless? And then, at dinner, she caught me staring.

She's like the sun when she smiles.

Dazzling. Bright. Bad for the eyes.

These feelings for Rae aren't right. I know this. I'm to leave our home one day and meet a woman who doesn't share my last name.

"There," Dad whispers, pointing toward a thick part of the woods.

I'm trying to pay attention to the potential game we're stalking, but I'm lost inside my own head. Last night, I stroked my cock, imagining Rae's mouth on me. I came so hard I saw stars. Then, this morning, before we left, I came again with thoughts of us naked and in bed, my cock deep inside her.

It can't ever happen, but that doesn't stop the maddening images from assaulting me at every turn. I want to tell Ronan, just so I don't have to bear this secret alone, but how do I even admit that shit?

Yip.

"Stay here," Dad instructs.

Dad prowls toward the sound, shotgun raised and

at the ready. When he reaches the source, he lowers his weapon.

"Goddammit."

Raegan rushes forward and I follow after her. The grisly scene before us is gut-churning. A full-sized wolf is mutilated, having clearly been on the losing side of a fight with a bear. Three wolf pups are also mangled and dead. Two, however, whimper and whine as they paw at the remains of their family.

"I need to put them out of their misery," Dad grumbles, aiming his shotgun at the white furball that's covered in blood.

"No!" Raegan shrieks. "They're just babies."

"Babies with no mother," Dad says, sighing. "It's cruel to leave them here motherless, sunshine."

The other pup, dark gray and also sticky with blood, attempts to nurse from its dead mother to no avail. My heart sinks. He's right. We should put them out of their misery.

But seeing the heartbroken expression on my sister's beautiful, slightly freckled face is too much to bear. I want to see her smile again.

"We could look after them," I tell him. "We can't let them die, Dad."

Raegan nods, ponytail bouncing. "Please, Daddy. Please don't kill them."

Dad groans and squats to pick the hungry pup up by the scruff of its neck. It howls and squirms in his grip. "They're wild animals."

"Babies. They're babies," Raegan argues. "We have to take care of them. It's the right thing to do."

"We can't keep them." Dad shakes his head, thrusting the whimpering pup at us. "This will turn into that." He motions with the pup to the mangled mother. "Then they'll hurt *you*."

Raegan stomps forward and takes hold of the pup, pulling it to her chest. "I'll train them to be good, Dad. You won't let me have my own cabin. Let me have this."

His lips thin out, and for a moment I think he'll deny her, but then he sighs in resignation. "They're not allowed in the big house. The second one of them even looks at any of the kids wrong or so much as growls at them, I'll put a bullet in their heads."

The gray pup yelps in Raegan's arms. When its soulful blue eyes meet mine, my heart squeezes.

"Come here, little one," I say as I set my weapon down to take the pup. "Don't be afraid."

Normally, Raegan would throw a fit if I tried taking something from her—our favorite knife being proof— but not now. Not in this moment.

She smiles.

Again, I'm transfixed by the beauty of it. Her lips are full and a perfect rosy color that I can't seem to get out of my head no matter how hard I try. Brown eyes, which so often are narrowed at me, are wide and twinkling.

I like this smile on her and that she's easily gifting it to me.

She steps forward, her lovely pine scent enveloping

me, and gently eases the pup into my waiting hands. Silky, delicate fingers brush over mine, sending heat prickling over my flesh. A warm blush creeps over my cheeks. I force my gaze from her onto the pup, stroking its messy fur in what I hope is a comforting manner.

"You're safe now…" I frown at the pup, lifting him up briefly so I can check his sex. "You need a name, little fella."

"Mage," Raegan says. "The white one is Spirit. I already named them after characters in the book I'm reading."

Mage and Spirit.

I grin at her. "That's perfect."

Dad grunts, pointing north. "I'm going to continue to hunt. The two of you need to take the pups back home. Bathe them. Figure out a way to feed them. Make sure they stay warm. They'll probably die, though, without their mother."

"They won't die," I say with a fierceness I feel in my bones. "Will you, Mage?"

Mage gnaws at my jacket, mistaking the button for a nipple. He doesn't appear to be frail or weak. This wolf pup is just hungry.

Rae picks up the other pup, Spirit, and comes to stand beside me. She radiates happiness. The rays of her smile warm my flesh. I want to close my eyes and lean toward her, feeling her pleasure tickle over my skin.

I pick up my gun and then start trekking toward home. Rae settles into step beside me, whispering to

Spirit in a sweet voice that I don't hear often. It feels right being with her, doing something together. On the same side for once.

"One of the kids will probably try to steal Spirit," Rae grumbles. "She's quiet and sweet." She cuts her eyes over to me. "Then I'll have to steal Mage back."

The pups are brother and sister.

It's fitting a pair of siblings are their saviors.

I smirk at her. "You don't have your own cabin. But you can come over to visit me and Mage anytime you want."

Her smile widens. "Really? Do I have to knock?"

It's on the tip of my tongue to tell her she has to because the last thing I need is for her to catch me jerking off while moaning her name. Fuck no.

I can't exactly tell her no, though, without ruining this rare time of peace between us.

"Knock five times so I know it's you," I instruct, "and then count to twenty."

"A secret knock to enter your cabin?"

"Yeah. Our little secret."

She nods, pleased with that answer. At least twenty seconds will buy me enough time to put my dick away.

Three days later...

It wasn't one of the kids who stole Spirit, but Rowdy

instead. Spirit took to our older brother much like Mage has taken to me.

To say Raegan is pissed is an understatement. And, in the past, I took great pleasure in teasing her, but things are changing when it comes to her. It's growing more and more difficult to ignore my feelings.

A light rapping on my door indicates a visitor. Ronan. My older brother respects my privacy and doesn't spend all hours of every day trying to rile me up like Rae does. He's quiet and a good listener. Probably why, in a family full of big mouths, he's the favorite. Now more than ever, I wish I could confess to him this shit I'm dealing with. Of all people, Ronan would never divulge my secrets.

But I'm having a hard time admitting them to my-self, though.

Telling Ronan sounds like an impossibility.

"Come in," I call out, making Mage jolt.

The little wolf pup is sweet and cuddly, though Dad says he won't be that way for long. He's a predator and one day I might have to put him down if he seems like he might be a threat. I understand where Dad is com-ing from, and I'd do anything to protect my family, but I hope to God that day never comes.

Raegan adores Mage and would murder me in my sleep if I hurt him.

My cabin door opens and Ronan steps inside. He's a little taller than me by maybe an inch, but I'm by far bulkier. If Ronan can avoid it, he stays out of the woods and locked up in his own cabin, nose lost in one of his sci-fi novels. I never understood how he could read about adventures when so many lie just outside our doorstep.

"Come to see the pup?" I ask, grinning at him. "He's lazy like you."

Ronan smirks as he saunters over to where I'm sprawled out on the sofa, Mage snuggled against my chest. "Ha. Says the guy practically asleep in the middle of the day. I'm surprised you're not out hunting."

"Same reason you aren't," I grumble, not bothering to flip him off as he sits beside me. "Dad's trying to knock some sense into Rowdy."

Ronan nods and watches Mage snooze, but doesn't make to grab for him like Raegan would if she were here. "Rowdy's not happy about Uncle Atticus and his brood coming out to visit soon."

"What do you think happened? It's been like four years since Rowdy went out there to stay." I frown, searching my brother's face that resembles Raegan's more than I've ever noticed before until this moment.

He takes a second to respond, brows scrunching as he thinks about his answer. Facial features are where the similarities with Raegan and Ronan end. Ronan doesn't blurt out whatever is on his mind, consequences be damned like Raegan does.

"Not sure," Ronan admits with a sigh. "It had to be Wild, though."

I like Wild, mainly because Raegan hates him.

Ronan likes him a lot more than I do. They're definitely better friends. It's annoying, not because I want Wild to be my bestie or some shit, but because of how Ronan hangs on his every word when he's here, soaking up whatever crazy tale Wild has for us.

"You think Wild kicked his ass or something?" I ask, mulling over that idea in my head. "He plays football and benches a lot." Not that I really understand what either of those things mean, just that Wild brags about them whenever he's around.

Ronan shrugs and pushes his glasses up his nose. "Rowdy is bigger and definitely would've been four years ago. Wild never mentions why Rowdy is mad whenever we talk, so I don't really know. More likely, he said something super offensive to our brother."

Rowdy used to be cool when we were younger. Whatever happened when he went away definitely changed him and not for the better. I'm about to suggest we try to get the information out of Rowdy before Wild and his family come to visit when someone knocks on the door.

Knock. Knock. Knock. Knock. Knock.

Five times.

And twenty seconds later…

In steps the person who has me all twisted. *Raegan.*

I guess before I try and figure out Rowdy and Wild's shit, I better sort out my own.

CHAPTER FIVE

raegan

I T FEELS REALLY GOOD KNOWING I HAVE A SECRET knock to let me into Ryder's place. The feeling dissipates, giving way to annoyance to see Ronan and Ryder hanging out without me. No matter how hard I try, I always feel like an outsider when the two of them are together.

Is that how Ryder feels when I read books on Ronan's bed with him?

Guilt niggles at me, but I quickly squash it in favor of taking my pup from my brother. Ryder avoids eye contact as he passes Mage to me. The wolf pup has been a great distraction from what happened just a few days ago.

My skin prickles at the memory of Ryder's cock getting hard. At first I thought it was funny to tease him about it, but after watching my parents together, lost in pleasure, my mind has twisted my thoughts into something shameful.

"Mom's freaking out," I say, ignoring the way my cheeks burn hot. "She's cleaning the house from top to bottom. I had to get out of there."

Ryder snorts. "I'm surprised she wasn't making you help."

"She was," I mumble, kissing Mage's furry head. "I'm supposed to be cleaning the bathroom. I tiptoed out of there as soon as she got distracted by Dawson."

"She'll be pissed when she finds out you're gone," Ryder says, grinning at me. "Then you'll be forced to do more chores."

Considering Dawson had a blowout in his diaper that leaked through the cloth and got all over his bedding, I'd say she'll be busy for a while before she'll miss me.

"She can do them herself," I sass back, keeping my voice down in case Dad happens to be lurking nearby.

"Rae," Ronan admonishes, eyes wide behind his glasses. "Be nice."

I crumple at his words, my heart squeezing with a well-timed ache. "Maybe she should be nice for once."

"I don't know why she's so hard on you," Ryder says, shockingly agreeing with me. "She tries so hard to protect you, but it's like she's blind to the fact she should be protecting everyone else *from* you."

"You had to ruin it," I growl, flipping him off. "And she better protect Wild from me when he shows up. I'll sic Mage on him."

Ryder laughs and Ronan shakes his head in exasperation.

"It's warm out today," I say, glancing between them. "Might be the last warm day we get now that summer is nearly over. Want to go for a swim?"

"Water's too cold," Ronan replies with a frown. "We'll freeze."

I'd looked at the thermometer on the porch of the big house earlier, and it'd read sixty-seven degrees in the heat of the day. Tonight, it'll probably get down to the mid-forties. But it's still a heck of a lot warmer than it'll be in just a couple more weeks. Where we live in Alaska, it starts cooling down in August, and by September, it's chilly a lot of the time. We seriously probably won't get another chance until next summer.

"I'll warm you up," I tease. "Come on. Don't be a loser."

My taunts don't ever work on Ronan the way they do on Ryder. Luckily, my adrenaline-junkie brother takes my side.

"Yeah, *lose*r, we'll warm you up if you get cold," Ryder says, hopping to his feet. "Let's go before we get roped into helping Mom clean shit off Dawson."

Ronan groans but concedes, also standing up. I squeal in delight, making Mage yelp in fright.

"Last one there has to finish cleaning the bathroom," I yell, already darting toward the door. "See you there, slow pokes."

Running through the wilderness never gets old. It's re-freshing to fill my lungs with pine-scented air and to hear twigs crackling under each step of my boots. Whenever I feel stifled or trapped by Mom in our loud house, I can count on running to fill my soul and reset my mind.

Ryder and Ronan both run after me but let me keep my lead. They both can be dicks when it comes to chores, so I have no doubt they'll pass me up right before we get to our swim hole—a narrow but deep creek about two miles away from our home.

The trail widens the closer we get to the creek and then it opens to a small clearing made of smooth, flat rocks. Before I can set Mage down and dive in, strong arms encircle my waist, making me scream so loud, several birds take off in flight.

Ryder's booming laugh rumbles through my back, boiling my blood. Ronan takes his sweet time removing his glasses, then undressing down to his underwear. He takes Mage from my arms and then sets the pup down before diving into the creek. When he pops up, he lets out an inhuman shriek.

"Holy fuck, it's cold!"

I fight against Ryder's hold, determined not to have to clean that damn bathroom, but fail miserably because Ryder has muscles for days. Trying a different tactic, I press my ass against his penis. I let out a triumphant howl of laughter when his whole body stiffens and he pulls his hips back in an effort to hide where else he's stiff.

I'm about to wriggle free when I'm reminded about this morning, way before the sun came up, how I touched myself shamelessly. I'd been thinking of how Ryder had been between my thighs when he got hard. Just like Dad was when he was thrusting into Mom. My usual fantasies of Ronan were replaced by Ryder instead.

I realize neither of us is moving, both frozen aside from the way our chests heave from exertion. Warmth tickles over my flesh.

"Let go of me," I say breathlessly, once again pushing my ass against him. "You're hurting me."

The animalistic groan that escapes him when my ass meets his hard penis indicates *I'm* the one hurting *him*. But after what Ronan told me and then what I saw with my parents, I know Ryder isn't sick or hurt. This feels good to him. *I* feel good to him.

"Stop moving," Ryder hisses, face pressed into my shoulder. "Fuck, just stop moving and I'll let you go."

His hot breath tickles my skin through my shirt and I shiver. The second he lets go of me, I'll bolt to the creek. But he doesn't let me go. With no warning, he lifts me off the ground and takes off in a sprint. He twists his body as we go into the creek, taking the brunt of the fall with his back.

As soon as the icy creek water touches my skin and then submerges me, I lose all thought as the cold annihilates me. Ryder releases me so we can both swim to the surface. I suck in a lungful of air and am about to let him have it when he grins brightly at me.

"You lose. I hit the water first," Ryder says in a smug tone. "Sucks being you."

I splash him and then try to dunk him. Ronan, ever the peacemaker, grabs hold of my arm, drawing me away from Ryder.

"You could have at least given me a chance to get out of my clothes," I snap at Ryder. "You're a prick."

He snorts, unperturbed by my insults. I shoot Ronan a sour look for not having my back before pulling my arm free. I swim to the creek bank and splash out of the water. Mage has found a warm rock to curl up on and watches us with a cocked head.

My brothers cut up and toss each other around while I peel my soaked jeans and boots off. Swimming in nothing but my bra and panties isn't uncommon for us ever since we got in trouble for skinny-dipping, but for some reason, today I'm aware of my naked skin.

I hesitate before pulling my shirt off, wondering why I'm hit with sudden awkwardness.

Slap!

Ryder's soaked shirt smacks me right in the back of the head. Asshole! I rip off my shirt and then throw myself back into the creek with one mission.

Kill Ryder.

He grabs hold of Ronan's shoulders, using him as a human shield. I reach my arms around Ronan in an attempt to punch Ryder right on that stupid laughing mouth of his. Ronan grabs onto my hips to keep me from getting to our brother. His strong but gentle fingers press into my chilled flesh and I suck in a sharp breath.

Distracted, and no longer interested in exacting revenge, I draw my gaze to Ronan. His dripping hair hangs in his eyes as he smirks at me. Heat travels down my spine, pooling in my core. I grow transfixed by his full, pink lips. They're so slick and soft looking. I bet they'd feel softer than my fingers on my pussy.

A shudder ripples through me and my teeth clack together. Confusing the reason for my shaking, Ronan pulls me to him, crushing me into his solid chest. My breasts smush against his pectoral muscles, making my heart race.

If I wrapped my legs around him, would his penis get hard too?

Would he thrust inside of me like Dad did with Mom, possessive and claiming?

All of our squealing and yelling are silenced. I tear my gaze from Ronan's to see what has Ryder so quiet. He's now treading the water behind Ronan, glowering at me.

What's his problem?

I'm the one who's supposed to be mad.

"What?" I snap, meeting Ryder's glare. "You don't get to be angry. You're the one who cheated, not me."

Ryder's jaw clenches and his eyes turn stormy. He dunks under the water and when he resurfaces, he's on the other side of the creek. I watch with a frown as he stomps out of the water. His jeans strain over his muscular thighs, but he's no longer hard from earlier.

Ronan turns us so he can see what Ryder's up to. He tries to extract me from his body, but I tighten my hold, wrapping my legs around his waist. Finally, he gives up on tugging me away, though he's not about to give up on making peace.

"Ry," he calls out. "What's wrong?"

Ryder's hands land on his hips as he stares off into the woods. The scar along his shoulder blade on the right side shimmers in the late afternoon light. He actually got that scar from one of the rocks in this creek when horsing around one time.

"He's just mad he got hard again," I whisper to Ronan. "Not my fault he wants to get me pregnant."

Ronan flinches, snapping his head back to me. "Rae. What the fuck?"

Not one to be chastised by my siblings, I shrug, unaffected. "It's true. I felt it."

Something akin to pain flickers in Ronan's brown eyes, making me instantly hate myself for revealing Ryder's secret. Again.

"You're going to get him in trouble," Ronan mutters, irritation in his tone. "Why can't you let up on him just once?"

Now it's my time to hurt. My chest burns deep in my heart when his words stab into me. Ronan is my best friend. We don't fight. Ever. Yet, he's mad at me.

I swallow down my emotion, releasing my hold on

him, and swim backward toward the creek bank. Ryder has disappeared into the trees, probably to take a piss or to pout or both.

"This was supposed to be fun," I gripe as I slosh my way out of the frigid creek. "Turns out, cleaning the bathroom would have been a lot better. At least no one at home tries to drown me or yell at me."

So much for having one last day to enjoy a rare warm day and swim before cold weather is indefinitely up on us until spring.

"Rae, wait," Ronan calls after me. "I didn't yell. I just—"

"Some friend you are," I bite back. "Maybe I will go live with Uncle Atticus and Aunt Eve. Then I wouldn't have to deal with you two idiots."

My mean, cruel words are sour on my tongue, but when I'm angry, I can't keep my mouth shut. Usually, Ryder is on the receiving end. Today, Ronan gets that wrath.

I bend over to grab my shirt when I get a crawling sensation of someone watching me. Ronan is watching me, but I'm not weirded out by him. This is something else—*someone* else.

Two boys come into view on our well-worn path, staring at me with wide eyes of shock.

Who the hell are these people?

CHAPTER SIX

ronan

Without my glasses, I can't see why Raegan's retreating form suddenly stops. Her fury is replaced by fear so potent I can almost taste it.

"Ryder!" I bellow, hoping like hell I don't agitate the bear or whatever it is that's scared Rae.

Leaves crunch behind me and then my brother curses. "Ro, get out of the water. Now."

I wade toward the creek bank, grateful to hear Ryder splashing behind me. Just as I grab my glasses and slide them on my face, I hear voices.

Not a bear.

People.

Two guys, a little older than me and Ryder, are gaping at my sister like they can't believe she exists. It takes me all of three seconds to realize she's standing there in nothing but her underwear that clings to every curve.

THE UNTAMED

"Clothes on. Now," Ryder growls, sounding very much like our father.

"You're on private property," I sputter out. It's something Dad always starts with on the rare occasion we've run into other people who don't belong here. Those words are usually enough to send them scampering away for good.

These guys don't flinch or bother tearing their interested stares from Rae. Thankfully, Ryder is still half-clothed and steps in front of her. I hastily throw on my clothes, which spurs Rae into action to do the same.

"You heard him," Ryder barks out. "This is private property. We own this land and you're trespassing."

Stupidly, none of us brought any weapons, too eager to play.

Dad will kill us once he finds out.

If these guys don't kill us first.

Glancing around, I look for anything that could be used for a weapon. Dad says people traipsing around in the woods are bad and have no reason to be here except running from the law. People in these woods are dangerous.

We were so careless, we fell into their trap.

I snatch up a fallen tree branch that's big enough to hurt if used as a weapon. One of the guys, who's covered all over in freckles and has offensive orangish-colored hair, eyes the branch warily. He elbows the guy next to him, drawing his attention to me as well.

Freckle Guy speaks up as he lifts both palms in the

air. "We're just passing through. Didn't mean to scare you."

The other guy, possibly his brother since their features are similar, nods in agreement. His brows lift and I notice a scar running through one of them. "We're not here to hurt you."

Despite their words, I grip my branch tighter, taking a threatening step forward. I may not be as good as Ryder at most things outdoors, but I can defend myself and my family. Right now, I'm our only hope as I have a weapon.

"Leave," I growl. "Leave before my dad shoots your heads off your shoulders."

The guys grimace at my words. Movement in the corner of my eye tells me Raegan is now dressed, which makes me breathe a little easier knowing she can run if I need her to.

"Listen," Scar Brow says, a playful lilt on his lips. "We're here with our family and a couple others. Me and Jace went exploring after we set up camp. Totally didn't expect to run into anyone." He thrusts a hand toward Ryder. "I'm CJ."

In the city, people shake hands. I've seen Dad and Atticus do it many times as a greeting. But they're friends. These guys are trespassers.

"I'm Raegan," my sister chirps, stepping past Ryder. "Nice to meet you."

Before we can stop her, she shakes CJ's hand and then Jace's. Despite their efforts to be friendly, neither one can keep their eyes off her chest where her wet shirt clings to her breasts. Uneasiness tickles down my spine. I'm still not opposed to smacking them with my branch.

"These are Ryder and Ronan, my brothers," she continues, a bright smile on her face. "You really are trespassing, though, and if my dad were here, he'd shoot first and ask questions later."

Jace pales and CJ shifts on his feet, eyes darting into the woods. Good. They should be scared.

"I guess we're dead either way," CJ says with a groan. "When our dads find out we freaked out the owners of this property, they're going to strangle us."

"Not really," Jace spits out quickly, frowning at CJ. "My cousin is dramatic."

"I know we're like the enemy or whatever," CJ jokes, grinning at us, "but my sister would die to meet you all. She's bored out of her skull. I'd say she's around your age, Raegan."

"Seventeen?"

"Almost," CJ confirms. "I called it. Me and Jace are both twenty-one."

"In town, we're allowed to buy liquor. Legally." Jace waggles his orange eyebrows at us. He slides the strap of his backpack off one shoulder and unzips it, pulling out a bottle of brown liquor like the kind Atticus brings Dad. "Lucky for you guys, we like to share."

The guys haven't tried to beat us up or shoot us or anything crazy. Maybe we're just overreacting.

"We're not allowed to drink," I grumble. "Only Rowdy is."

CJ arches his scarred brow, making it pucker in a strange way. "There are more kids? Any more girls?"

Ryder takes a step forward, crossing his arms over his strong, bare chest. These guys are fit, but they're nothing like Ryder, who looks seconds from slamming their heads together for entertainment.

"I think it's time for you to move along," Ryder grunts. "You do not want to meet our father."

Raegan huffs. "Don't be an ass, Ry. They're trying to be friendly and you're scaring them away."

"Promise we're not bad people," CJ, and clearly the spokesman of the two, assures us. "Plus, if we didn't act right, my momma would beat both of us with a switch. That woman is vicious."

Jace makes a silly face, nodding emphatically. "Aunt Tee once came after me with a frying pan! With the eggs still in it!"

Both guys snort with laughter at their seemingly fond memory.

"Why are you here on our land?" Ryder demands. "You say you're passing through, but we're smack dab in the center of our property and we own a lot of it. Are you trying to walk all the way to Canada? Why? What are you hiding?"

CJ frowns, darting a confused look my way. As if I'll save him from my brother. Fat chance, man.

"Look, we don't mean any harm." CJ takes the bottle

of liquor from his cousin and takes a swig. "We just get really bored, so finding people our age is the most exciting shit that's happened to us in forever."

Ryder takes another step forward, almost like he's going to accept the bottle, but stops short. He ripples with power, making both guys who are older than him flinch. "You didn't answer my questions," Ryder growls. "What are you hiding?"

Jace takes the liquor bottle and recaps it before letting out a heavy sigh. "Our dads are government conspiracy nuts. It's fucking embarrassing. They uprooted our families and dragged us off the grid. We're looking to settle someplace away from society. Haven't found anything yet. Each time we find someplace cool, people already live there."

"You lived in a town?" I ask, unable to hide my curiosity. "Where?"

"Seattle," CJ answers with a lopsided grin. "The city had a good party scene. Every weekend was fucking awesome. Girls, booze, pot."

"But our dads all but dragged us with them," Jace mutters. "We didn't put in a notice at our jobs or anything. Just picked up and left."

"You had a job?" Raegan asks. "Doing what?"

CJ laughs. "Nothing exciting. I was delivering pizzas while in college. Jace worked sometimes at the shoe store in the mall."

To emphasize CJ's claim, Jace shoots his foot out, showing off his hideously bright red shoe. "Twenty percent off employee discount. Man, those were the good ol' days."

Raegan, seemingly fine with our new "friends," saunters over to Jace and holds out her hand. "I don't know what an employee discount is, but I'll take a drink."

Before me or Ryder can stop her, she takes a long swallow of the amber liquid. Then she starts coughing. Both the guys crack up with laughter. I can't help but smirk and even Ryder relaxes his shoulders a bit.

"Can't handle your liquor?" Jace teases. "This stuff is stout, but when I was seventeen I was chugging this shit."

"That's because you're a fucking alcoholic, dumbass," CJ retorts with a grin. "Are we all cool? Because, if you don't care, we can take you over to meet our family. Mya will seriously kill me if I don't introduce you guys to her."

The dynamic between the cousins is relaxed and they both appear to be happy. Maybe we are overreacting. I let out a resigned sigh, tossing the branch onto the forest floor.

Jace hollers, fist pumping the air. "He's not going to kick our asses!"

Mage, having finally had enough of our antics, yips as if to tell us to shut up. Both of the guys jerk their heads to our wolf, who's still curled up on a rock, jaws unhinged.

"Do you have a wolf for a pet? Are you for real?" CJ asks in astonishment. "That's so badass."

Raegan saunters over to the pup and scoops him into her arms. "His name is Mage. He's my sweet boy."

"Technically, he's mine," Ryder interjects.

Oh, geez, here we go again.

"They'll go like this for hours," I mutter, shaking my head slightly. "And I do mean hours."

CJ chuckles. "You should hear me and Mya. Not a day goes by where one of us isn't nagging at the other. She turned into a total brat once she lost her phone and didn't have social media."

I know what social media is because Wild has it and uses it. Wild also has a phone, though it never works when he comes out to visit. Even unable to pick up a signal, I've always been impressed by the tiny device and Wild's extensive stash of nudes stored in the pictures.

Nudes of women, not himself.

A warm blush creeps over my skin. At least I don't find any of these guys attractive. Not like Wild and especially not like Ryder.

"Jace!" someone hollers in the distance. "Jace!"

Jace tilts his head back, staring up at the tree canopy, and groans. "My brother lives to make me miserable." He huffs before bringing his chin back down. "I swear if he could magically become my dad, he'd try to. It's annoying as fuck."

A man appears in the clearing behind Jace and CJ. As he approaches, my hackles rise again, knowing we no longer outnumber the newcomers, but are evenly matched now in numbers. The man's eyes are green like the moss-covered rocks near the river, but not at all playful like that of Jace's. He darts his stare over me and my siblings, his full mouth thinning into a hard line.

"Friends," Jace mutters, "meet my brother, Logan. Logan, this is Ryder, Raegan, and Ronan."

Logan's attention bounces to each one of us as we're introduced before lingering on me. He takes the time to swoop his gaze over my entire form before landing on my lips. Heat floods my cheeks.

He probably has at least ten years on Jace, putting him in his early thirties. Unlike Jace, Logan has just a few freckles on his cheeks above his trimmed mahogany-colored beard. Sunlight makes a few of the hairs glisten like gold. He's a lot more solid than Jace, putting him closer to Ryder's size.

It's hard to ignore, but he's quite beautiful.

"Nice to meet you," Logan says to us, voice tight with tension. "What are you kids doing out here?"

Kids?

"I'm nineteen," I blurt out, hating how my face burns hot. "I'm not a kid."

Logan arches a brow and then his lips curl into a lopsided grin that makes my heart flutter. "Duly noted, Ronan. A man, not a boy."

Ryder shoots me a questioning look over his shoulder, but I refuse to look at him. I barely understand my own feelings—for men, no less—so I don't have the capacity to explain my reaction to my brother.

"Dad's looking for you," Logan says to Jace. "You can run along back to camp now."

Jace scoffs. "I found them first."

Logan stiffens but ultimately ignores Jace in the end. He flashes me a disarming grin as he scratches his beard. "You'll have to excuse my brother and cousin. They're always looking for friends. My father doesn't trust people well, so it's up to me to look out for those two."

A breath rushes past my lips and I nod at his words. "Our dad isn't all that trusting either. Sounds like they may get along."

"Then let's have them meet," Logan says, his smile widening. "It's a date."

I'm not sure if it's the words or the way he winks at me after.

Either way, I find myself nodding and agreeing to what will no doubt get my ass handed to me by my father.

Smile. *It's a date.* Wink.

Whatever trouble I just landed myself in will be worth it.

CHAPTER SEVEN

ryder

HAVE MY SIBLINGS LOST THEIR MINDS? BOTH Ronan and Raegan seem to have forgotten everything Dad has taught us. Most importantly: Never trust strangers.

Yet…

They both are happy about these new people invading our land. Sure, they're charming and a bit comical, but I'm not completely sold. And I know Dad sure as hell wouldn't be. That's why it's my job to protect them from these trespassers.

"No," I grind out, ignoring the sharp looks my siblings give me. "Not happening. Time for us to part ways."

Raegan opens her mouth to argue, but I shoot her a nasty glare that has her stopping short. I'll throw her over my shoulder and drag her ass home if I have to.

"Ry," Ronan mutters, a slight plead to his voice. "We don't have to be rude. Maybe Dad will—"

"No," I snap, turning my anger on him. "This isn't up for discussion."

Ronan flinches at my harsh words, making me feel like a total dick. Then he turns to look back over at Logan, his cheeks burning with embarrassment.

"I'm sorry," Ronan says to Logan. "I…I'm sorry."

Logan gives him a knowing smile and nod, accepting his words. Their little exchange lights a fire in my gut, burning hot with a mixture of jealousy and possessiveness.

Ronan is my brother. Some asshole doesn't get to swoop in and take him away from me.

"Let's go," I growl, snagging Ronan by his elbow. "You too, Rae."

Raegan's freckled cheeks are also red from humiliation. So sorry to be the voice of reason around here. They'll both get over it. She gives the guys a little wave before storming back toward the direction of home, Mage in her arms. I don't let go of Ronan as I swipe my shirt off the rock where I'd left it.

"I'd keep moving if I were you," I spit out to Logan since he's the apparent leader of the three. "Our land spans far and wide. Get off of it as quickly as you can."

Logan ignores me, watching Ronan intently as we pass. When Ronan jerks to a stop, I whip around to find Logan has snagged his wrist in his hand.

"It was a pleasure meeting you, Ronan. An absolute pleasure."

Ronan smiles—actually fucking grins—at this prick,

which infuriates me. A snarl escapes me as I jerk my brother along with me, tugging him from Logan's poisonous hold. My ears ring with anger as I storm through the woods, weaving our way along the familiar paths. I keep Raegan in my sight and refuse to let go of my brother, not that he's even attempting to pull away.

The voices from the three guys eventually can no longer be heard. I'm sure we've gone at least a mile—putting us halfway home—when Ronan finally speaks.

"Why?" he croaks out. "Why couldn't you let me make a friend?"

Raegan puts more distance between us, but I know she'll be fine now that the threat is literally behind us. I halt and turn to glower at Ronan.

"Those people were not friends."

His nostrils flare and his brown eyes flicker with anger. At me. Ronan never gets angry, especially not at me. Guilt swarms in my gut, making me second-guess my actions.

"They could have been," Ronan hisses, finally freeing his arm from my grip. "How are we expected to meet people and have families of our own one day if Dad never lets us talk to anyone?"

"They could have been lying about there being girls," I grumble. "It could have just been the three of them."

Ronan's cheeks burn bright red again, confusing me further. "Whatever. You made your point and it's over now. Opportunity wasted."

He stalks off toward home, leaving me behind. Why

is he so pissed? When it was just CJ and Jace, he was ready to clobber them with a branch. But when Logan showed up, he suddenly liked the trio. Makes no sense.

The walk back is a somber one. Raegan and Ronan go their separate ways once we're in the safety of our fenced-in yard. I know I should tell Dad about what happened. He'll be furious and rip my siblings a new one for trusting in them. Furthermore, I'll get my ass chewed out for leaving my weapons at home. That whole situation could have gone sideways so quickly.

Mom won't let Raegan ever leave her sight. No more hunting trips. No more swimming or hanging out with us from beyond our yard. If I tattle, she'll be trapped more so than she already is.

And Ronan?

The whole encounter with him and Logan leaves me feeling uneasy. I don't know exactly where it went weird, but I could feel it. Dad won't like what happened at all. Ronan will probably get the belt, despite being nineteen years old. You're never too old in this family to get an ass whipping for misbehaving.

I can't tell Dad if I want to keep my two favorite siblings from getting in trouble.

I won't tell.

I'm jittery as I step into the big house for supper. The house is loud as per usual, the baby howling, the little ones arguing, and Raegan yapping about Mage. Ronan, however, is somber. Guilt creeps up my spine. After our intense afternoon, we all went our separate ways until dinnertime. I'd wanted to make things right with both of them, but quite frankly didn't have the balls to deal with it.

"The bear is back," Rowdy states in a quiet voice before shoveling in a heaping forkful of potatoes that miraculously steer clear of his scraggly beard. "Momma grizz. Cub tracks too."

Dad, who'd been feeding Dawson, freezes and whips his head around to Rowdy. "You've been leaving food out again?"

"No," Rowdy grunts. "I don't know why they're interested in my cabin."

"It's time we build you your own cabin near your brothers," Dad grumbles, voice stern. "You're too far away for my liking anyway."

Rowdy's nostrils flare, but he nods. "Yes, sir."

I wait for Raegan to throw a fit about boys getting cabins and the unfairness of the female life, but she shockingly remains quiet. I'm sure she'll bitch about it to me and Ronan later.

"Can I help build your cabin?" Destiny asks, smiling toward the sound of Rowdy's voice.

"You can't see," Dakota reminds her and then makes a show of waving four fingers in the air near her face. "How many fingers am I holding up?"

"Kota," Mom admonishes. "Enough."

When she turns away, Dakota sticks his tongue out at her. That kid's a brat from hell. He's lucky Dad didn't see it or he'd be getting a well-deserved spanking.

"I can help," Destiny huffs. "I can, Rowdy."

Rowdy, a grouch to everyone else, gifts her a smile she can't even see. "I know you can, Dez. Thank you."

Destiny perks up and then holds up four fingers to Dakota. Lucky guess. It has Dakota frowning in confusion. Good. If he thinks she can really see, maybe he'll stop terrorizing his older sister.

The table descends into silence, which has me, Ronan, and Raegan stiffening guiltily. So much for not saying anything.

Mom and Dad exchange a worried look and then Dad's penetrating glare lands on me. Fuck. I shove a roll into my mouth—the whole damn thing—and chew like our goat, Fleabag, does with my mouth open and noisily.

Dad snaps his attention to Ronan. "Where did you all go this afternoon?"

Ronan shifts in his seat. "Huh?"

"What did you three do?" Mom asks, frowning my way. "You're all acting weird."

The second I finish swallowing my roll, Dad's stare is back on mine, daring me to chew my way through answering. I drop my fork on my plate with a clatter and then blurt out my answer. "We went swimming."

"I want to go swimming," Dakota whines. "Not fair!"

Declan, who's three and also loves swimming, starts whining, "Me swim too!"

Mom ignores them to probe more. "Swimming where? The river by Rowdy's?"

Raegan sits straight up and smiles sweetly at Mom. "The creek."

The creek where she and Ronan got caught swimming naked once. The creek we aren't supposed to go to. The swimming hole that's off-limits.

Fuck.

"Unbelievable," Mom cries out, voice shrill. "You three were told under no circumstances are you allowed to go back there."

"Mom, relax," Raegan sasses. "We kept our underwear on. No babies were made."

I cringe when Dad's hot glare is back on me.

"D-Dad, we didn't do anything bad," I stammer out. "It won't happen again."

He doesn't get to answer because Mom's voice has risen several octaves. "You're damn right it won't happen again. What were you all thinking? You're all getting to that age!"

"The age we want to have fun?" Raegan snaps back, challenging Mom with a glare. "Oh no, heaven forbid we enjoy our stupid lives for once!"

"Raegan," Dad roars, slamming a fist down onto the table, making everyone's glasses slosh. "That's enough, goddammit. You will not speak to your mother like that."

If they're this pissed about us swimming alone together, then they'll lose their shit altogether when they learn we met some trespassers. What's the big deal anyway if we swim together without supervision?

"You're not allowed to go anywhere alone with your brothers anymore, Sunshine. Sorry," Dad says, regret in his voice, "but that's the way it has to be."

Just like all our dinners, Raegan fights the hardest and the loudest, while the rest of us kids go silent. I just want this meal to be over so I can go back to my cabin and forget all this shit happened.

"So now I'll be trapped cooking and cleaning and babysitting in this stupid prison until I decide to let Wild get me pregnant? That's your vision for my life?" Raegan rises to her feet, sending her chair scraping across the wood floors. "Sorry, but I don't choose that life."

We all gape at Raegan's bold words.

She glances out the window and then she curls her lips from a sneer into a pretty smile. "I'll choose my own life and it's not Wild," she hisses. "I'm going to marry CJ."

Fuck. Fuck. Fuck.

"Who the hell is CJ?" Dad grinds out, confusion in his words.

"Looks like you get to meet him, Daddy."

CHAPTER EIGHT

raegan

"RAEGAN!"

Dad's booming voice behind me does nothing to deter me. Now that I've dug myself into some deep shit, there's no turning back. Literally.

I bolt out the front door, eager to meet my new friend and escape my parents' unfair rules.

CJ, alone and no longer with his cousin, grins when he sees me leap off the porch. My heart rate speeds up as my legs carry me right into his arms. Because I launch myself at him, he loses his balance and I tackle him to the ground.

"Happy to see me?" he teases, eyes twinkling.

I barely get to enjoy the view because a strong arm hooks around my chest and jerks me back. I'm physically shoved behind my father, who aims his .45 pistol at CJ's head.

CJ's no longer smiling.

"Whoa, man, whoa," CJ says, shooting a terrified look my way. "I know Raegan. She's my friend."

Dad tenses and then steps closer to CJ, who's making no moves to get to his feet. "Get the fuck off my property."

"Daddy!" I shriek, grabbing the back of his shirt. "Stop it!"

He doesn't turn to look at me or even attempt to shake me off. Ryder, Ronan, and Rowdy all show up seconds later. Rowdy is the only one with his gun drawn too. I shoot Ryder a pleading look to fix this before our new friend gets shot.

"Dad," Ryder mutters. "We, uh, kind of met them today at the creek."

"Them?" Dad growls, head lifting toward the open gate. "There're more?"

"They're not bad people," Ronan chimes in, starting toward the gate. "I swear."

Our parents are definitely going to kill us, but I don't care. I'm so sick of them keeping us trapped in their safe little box. I want to live and feel and experience things. I'm not like Mom. I don't want to be some stupid kept woman.

I want to be free.

Two familiar faces walk through the gate. Logan and Jace aren't carrying any weapons, which I'm grateful for or else I'm pretty sure Dad would have shot them dead on the spot.

"CJ," Logan says, eyeing his cousin on the ground. "What the hell are you doing, man?"

CJ barks out a harsh laugh. "I had to see her again."

Probably the wrong thing to say when my dad has a gun pointed at his face, but it makes my heart stutter in my chest. If I can't have Ronan like I secretly crave, some stranger who isn't Wild is fine by me. CJ and his family seem cool—a lot cooler than mine.

"Someone better start explaining fast," Dad snarls. "Before I start shooting."

"They're just passing through," I explain, pushing past Dad to give CJ my hand. "We ran into them while swimming. They're nice, Dad."

CJ allows me to pull him to his feet. I can practically feel Dad's rage burning hot against my back, but I don't care. He'll have to shoot through me to get to CJ and that'll never happen.

"My dad's a little overprotective," I tell CJ, smiling.

"A little?" CJ snorts out a laugh. "I'm CJ Greer, uh, sir."

He offers a hand to my dad, but he glowers at him. "I don't give a fuck who you are. I want you gone."

Logan, now with Ronan at his side and Jace on the other, slowly walk toward us.

"We'll leave," Logan says, holding his hands up in a placating way. "We'd be much obliged if you could point us in the right direction."

Dad doesn't breathe a word, waiting for Logan to continue.

Logan lets out a sharp breath. "My stepmom is pregnant. We're trying to find someplace to settle before Stacey has the baby."

I glance over my shoulder, wondering what my own mother thinks about that, but she's nowhere to be found. Knowing her, she probably has all the littles hidden away in the pantry. My parents are paranoid.

"This is our land," Dad growls. "Nowhere to settle around here."

"Understood," Logan says with a quick nod. "That's why we'll need a little direction. She's been having pains. Might be a little early for her to go into labor, but we're erring on the side of caution and looking for a place to set up camp for more than just a day or two."

"We're not a damn hospital," Dad says rudely.

"Daddy," I hiss. "Don't be cruel. She could die out there."

He ignores me, but I know it got to him because he finally lowers his weapon. Rowdy follows Dad's lead and holsters his as well.

"Got a map?" Dad asks in a gruff tone. "I can show you where to go."

Logan nods. "My dad and uncle have them. I'm going to call them."

Dad tenses when Logan reaches into his pocket. He pulls out a walkie-talkie—the same kind we got for Christmas one year from Uncle Atticus.

"Dad," Logan says into the device, "found CJ."

"Don't tell me he's bothering that family," the man

says on the other end. "We don't need any trouble with Stacey's state."

"I wish I could tell you otherwise, but your favorite nephew is all googly-eyed over their daughter." Logan snorts out a laugh. "Nearly got his ass shot in the face."

"Serves him right," the man grumbles. "How do we fix it? Will they let you all leave? Do we need to trade supplies or food for his freedom?"

"We could leave him as their prisoner," Logan offers, earning the middle finger from CJ.

"Tempting, but that won't do—"

His words are cut off by a woman crying out in pain.

"Stacey okay?" Logan demands, concern dripping from his words. "Is the baby coming?"

"Not sure," the man says wearily. "Just get your asses back to camp so we can take care of her. I'm afraid it won't be long before this baby gets here."

Dad surprises me when he lets out a resigned sigh and says, "Bring them here. They can stay outside the fence. We can give you a night or two of respite, direct you where to go next, and properly check out your woman."

Logan relays Dad's message to the man on the other end of the walkie-talkie.

"Can we trust these people?" the man asks. "I'm not looking to get my family raped and killed by crazy-ass bush people. We have little kids with us, Logan. Will they be safe?"

Sounds like he's just as paranoid as my dad.

"I think so," Logan says with a frown.

Ronan nods emphatically beside him. "We have kids here too. They'll be safe."

Logan flashes him a bright grin and then assures the man on the other end that it's okay to bring their people this way. After he gives him directions, he pockets the radio and begins chatting with Ronan.

I avoid my father, grab CJ's arm, and tug him over to where Ronan is. My heart flutters with excitement. What if these people are really cool? Maybe they could permanently build a camp nearby. It wouldn't be so boring and prison-like if we had more people to be around. Maybe I could get married and have my own life so I wouldn't have to follow my parents' rules.

"This is a pretty sweet setup you have here," Logan says to Ronan. "I think it'll give my father some ideas for when we finally settle somewhere."

Our setup *is* pretty sweet.

I'm certainly proud of our home.

Ronan pushes his glasses up his nose and shifts on his feet, cheeks turning a pretty pink color. I find myself fixating on his flushed skin, wondering what's up with that.

"I even have my own cabin," Ronan murmurs. "Over there. I'd be, uh, happy to show you or your dad or whomever."

I frown at my brother, confused at his awkwardness.

"All the boys around here get their own place," I

grumble to Logan. "If you're a girl, you just wait to get married off so you'll become someone else's problem."

Dad remains where he's at but doesn't miss my snarky words. "Raegan."

Ignoring his warning tone, I turn to CJ. "I may not have my own cabin, but I could show you my room."

CJ jerks his head toward my father, eyes wide with terror. "Eh, maybe that's a bad idea."

"Just a suggestion," I say sweetly.

Logan chuckles at our antics. "When CJ's dad, Owen, gets here, he won't let him out of his sight. These two knuckleheads are in a world of shit for approaching you guys back there at the creek. Sorry, sweetheart, but your attempt to piss off your father through my cousin won't be happening."

Ronan smirks at me. Now it's my turn to flush with humiliation. I'm used to Ryder driving me insane, but not Ronan. Never Ronan. Ever since he met Logan, it's like he's under the guy's spell, ready to make him his new best friend.

Jealousy prickles under my skin. I have the urge to step between Ronan and Logan but refrain, barely.

"Got any more of that liquor?" I mutter under my breath just loud enough for CJ to hear.

His grin is wolfish. "Jace does. Need a drink, pretty girl?"

I warm under his praise. He thinks I'm pretty. Besides Dad, I don't think anyone's ever called me pretty before. Certainly not Wild—my supposed "future husband."

"Badly," I say, smiling back. "Want to see our goat?" Then I raise my voice so my father can hear. "I'm going to show them Fleabag. Don't worry, you can still see me."

Dad's eyes narrow, but he gives me a slight nod. A thrill shivers down my spine knowing I finally, *finally* have gotten some freedom. Who knew? All I had to do was blow up and yell at everyone. Good to know for the future.

Ronan remains planted firmly at Logan's side, much to my annoyance, but as me, CJ, and Jace start toward Fleabag's pen, Ryder stalks toward us. So much for getting a moment away alone. I glower at my brother, warning him not to be an asshole. He gives me a flat, emotionless stare that boils my blood. Asshole it is.

"You guys really do have an awesome place," Jace says, gesturing at our fenced-in land. "I bet it sure beats sleeping in tents."

"Maybe you can stay," I suggest, ignoring Ryder's scoff. "Get on Dad's good side and I bet he would let you build nearby. He and Mom are grooming me to be a wife. Maybe I'll marry one of you two. Then they'll have to let you live near us."

"Dibs," CJ says, cackling with laughter. "I saw you first."

Plus, he called me pretty girl.

"You can both court me," I tease, grinning at CJ.

"This isn't a dumb historical romance novel," Ryder growls. "Stop being so careless and stupid."

His words hurt, but I don't let it show. I pretend he didn't even speak, choosing to run ahead to Fleabag's pen. Our goat is gray and loud like the rest of our family. She bleats upon our arrival, eager to see us.

I reach over the fencing around the pen to scratch her head before motioning for the guys to follow me to the other side of Fleabag's house. Leaning up against the back side of it, I stare off toward the wooden fence that keeps our property safe.

"We'll have to be discreet," I say, urging CJ to come stand beside me. "Don't let my dad see the bottle."

Jace and CJ sidle up beside me and then Jace slides the bottle my way. I sneak a drink and then sputter on the nasty liquid, once again earning me laughter from the guys.

Well, not Ryder.

He comes to stand directly in front of me, arms crossed over his chest, watching me through narrowed eyes. Maybe CJ's sister, Mya, will interest him and distract him from being a prick. He can get his penis hard all he wants and make a million babies with her. I'm sure my parents will be so proud since that's all they care about.

CJ nudges his thigh against mine, making goose bumps rise along my skin. He leans near me, his hot breath tickling my neck. "I'm glad I found you in the woods, pretty girl."

I melt at his words.

"Me too," I say, flashing him a small smile.

I make the mistake of looking at my brother, who vibrates with anger. His nostrils flare and he loudly cracks his neck, all in some stupid show to scare off my new friends.

Luckily, CJ is oblivious to Ryder.

If he can pretend my brother doesn't exist, I can too.

CHAPTER NINE

ronan

"THERE ARE A LOT OF GRIZZLIES AROUND THIS part," Dad grunts to Logan. "Your people would do well to remember that."

Logan, with his muscular arms crossed over his chest, nods at my father. "Appreciate the heads-up. We do what we can, but until we make a permanent settlement somewhere, we're pretty exposed. It's the children we worry about most."

If that was Dad's hint to offer them to stay within the fenced boundary, it went ignored. I suppress a sigh. My father doesn't like people and the mention of children does nothing for his barricaded heart.

"We have some bear spray," Rowdy offers. "More coming soon."

Of course I know his cryptic answer means Uncle Atticus will be here soon, but Logan doesn't know what to make of it.

"We'll happily take you up on that offer." Logan

cocks his head as if listening for something. "Might even trade you one of the screaming toddlers from our group."

Sure enough, we hear the screams of a child in the distance, no doubt the screaming toddler in question. Logan smirks at me, making sure I know he's joking and not actually into human trafficking. I flash him a bright grin back.

While we wait for his people, Dad discusses where they can fetch some fresh water—down at the river. Our own rainwater collection and filtration system goes unmentioned. I guess Dad's hospitality only goes so far.

"How'd you get all of this stuff?" Logan asks, gesturing toward the house, garden, and shed. "Looks like you have a fully functioning homestead. It's not cheap nor something you can easily scrape together by scavenging mismatched materials. Those solar panels are top of the line."

Dad bristles, not bothering to follow Logan's critical stare to our rooftop. "I have money and means."

Oh my God.

Dad is being insufferable and unwelcoming. Normally, I'm not one to step in and challenge my father, but since Ryder nor Raegan are around, someone has to do it.

"We have family in town. They bring us the supplies we need and check in on us from time to time." I ignore both Rowdy's and Dad's glowering for my oversharing.

"We give them a list and the next time they visit, they bring whatever we ask for."

Logan cuts his eyes my way again, lips quirking on one side. I try to look away from his mouth, but it's hard. I'm not an idiot or blind—well, not with my glasses at least—and can tell there's something sparking between us.

"You really do have the ideal home here," Logan says with a whistle of appreciation. "When we finally find our forever home, we hope to make it as nice as this. Who knows, if we're not too far away, maybe we could even set up some sort of trade system."

I cringe because I know Dad's answer before he even says it.

"In case you misunderstood, I own the land as far as the eye can see in every direction and then some." Dad ripples with irritation. "Unless you're prepared to travel weeks to trade game for goat cheese, I'd say it looks like you'll be on your own."

Logan takes it in stride, not getting insulted. He flashes me another quick wink that has my blood running hot and straight south to my dick. Casually, I thread my fingers together and let them rest in front of my crotch so no one sees just how much this man affects me. Logan slightly lifts a brow, not oblivious like my father and brother, and smiles.

To everyone around us, it's a friendly smile, but I see the dark, filthy glint in his eyes that promises more.

Holy shit.

Logan is into me. He's really into me and it's not a case of wishful thinking on my part. The urge to escape somewhere quiet with him is overwhelming. Would he kiss me? Would he work his large hand into my pants and stroke my cock?

I stifle a groan, only picking up pieces of the conversation that's continued without me. They're discussing the first snow of the year. Not a topic I even care about. I'd much rather daydream of ways to get Logan's smiling lips around my dick.

A whistle, sharp and loud, pierces the air just outside the fence. Logan whistles back, three times in quick succession. Then, two men step through the gate. Dad and Rowdy tense, weapons ready if need be. The two men see Logan and nod, ambling their way toward us. As they approach, I can tell the one with ruddy dark red hair with streaks of silver is Logan and Jace's dad while the man with auburn hair and the same silver on his head must be CJ's dad. Opposite of their children, the two men don't wear playful smiles.

Wariness of my family and their guns has them frowning. Both men are tense but don't draw their own weapons or turn around and run.

"Michael Greer," the one I'd pegged as Logan's dad says. "I see you've met my sons, Logan and Jace." He claps a hand on the other man's shoulder. "This here is my younger brother, Owen, father of that little shit over there."

CJ being the little shit in question.

"Reed Jamison," Dad grunts. "My sons Rowdy and Ronan. The other two over there are Raegan and Ryder."

Owen sighs in exasperation. "I see my son's already in love."

Dad ignores him, getting straight to business. "You have a woman who's in labor?"

"My wife, Stacey," Michael says, nodding. "Since she's only seven months, I sure as hell hope not. We've been walking for weeks, not stopping to camp but a night or two. I'm hoping she's just tired and suffering from Braxton Hicks. The alternative is scary as fuck. Considering you have four kids, I'd say you know the worry of childbirth in the wild with no medical assistance."

"Eight," I chime in, refusing to look at Dad or Rowdy and the daggers they shoot my way. "There are eight of us kids."

"Damn." Michael whistles. "I guess it's safe to say you know a thing or two about delivering babies."

Dad gives him a brief nod. "Where is she?"

Michael and Owen both tense. It's safe to say they're just as untrusting of us as we are of them. Owen scans the yard, clearly looking for threats, but then relaxes when he doesn't find anyone lurking.

"The others are nearby," Owen replies. "Don't want to overstep our welcome." His gaze falls on Fleabag braying from the goat pen. "I know a couple of little ones, though, who would be thrilled to see that goat."

"How many people are in your camp?" Dad asks, still not giving an inch to these people.

"We're up to twenty-eight now—" Michael's words are cut short when a kid, maybe five or six, comes barreling through the gate.

"Goat!"

A woman, not much older than Rowdy, with long, curly, auburn hair chases after the kid. She snags him up before he reaches the gate. When she turns to us, her face is bright red and she's equal parts embarrassed and terrified. The latter makes me feel like shit.

We're not bad people.

Dad just likes scaring others into thinking that's true.

"Hellie," Michael calls out. "Come say hello to Mr. Jamison, who's so kind as to allow us on his land."

With the little one's hand tightly clasped in hers, she approaches, eyeing my brother and father warily. I want to assure her no one here would hurt her, but Dad actually beats me to the punch.

"Reed," he says, offering a hand for Hellie to shake. "Who's this little guy?"

"I'm Nicky," the kid says. "Can I play with your goat?"

"I'll do you one better," Dad replies, finally relaxing. "I'll bring my son Dakota out. He's almost six. I'm sure he can show you all sorts of cool stuff." Then, to Michael, he says, "Go get your wife. I'll get mine. We'll see if we can't make her more comfortable."

Logan shoots me a triumphant grin.

This is going to be fun.

Us Jamison kids are long overdue for some fun.

"This place is mine," I tell Logan as we step inside my cabin. Alone. "Ugh, it's not that special."

They've been here for a couple of hours now, setting up camp just outside, and their people coming inside the gate to check out our property. There are a lot of them, but they all seem nice. Lots of children too, about seven of which are under the age of ten, which makes all of my younger siblings thrilled beyond belief. As much as I like seeing all the new faces, I'm thankful for stealing away with Logan by ourselves.

Logan walks over to my floor-to-ceiling bookshelf that takes up an entire wall. "I beg to differ. This cabin is fucking awesome."

Pride fills my chest and I let out a relieved breath. "I guess it kind of is."

"You read all these?" Logan asks as he tugs a book off the shelf and eyes me over his shoulder.

"Most, yeah. Some I didn't finish because they were boring or more Raegan's preference, but some of those books I've read many, many times. Like the one in your hand."

It was hidden up top, much different than the ones

Raegan reads and out of her reach. Dad would kill me if she ever got her hands on it.

He takes a closer look at the book. "Romance book with aliens?"

"Yeah." Heat floods my cheeks. "I just like them. I've read that entire series a bunch. Especially that book."

"Interesting." He flips through the book, landing on a dog-eared page. "This male alien is sucking another alien's cock."

I freeze, unable to formulate an answer. My skin prickles with shame.

"This is hot," Logan murmurs. "No wonder you like this one so much. Can I borrow it?"

"Y-Yeah," I stammer, barking out an awkward laugh. "Take whatever you want."

Logan turns, eyeing me with that filthy glint in his stare once more. His moss green eyes are easy to get lost in. He takes a step toward me and I nearly stumble over my own feet, needing to escape his intensity. It's too much. If he gets any closer, I might literally come in my pants just from anticipation.

"Take whatever I want," Logan murmurs and then bites down on one corner of his bottom lip. "Well, aren't you a gracious host." Another wink that burns a trail of heat straight to my dick.

The air is charged between us. I'm completely out of my element here, but I'm here for it. All of my fantasies I've had of Wild and Ryder both dissipate in favor of letting reality take over.

This is happening.

Logan Greer is flirting with me.

A hot, charismatic, strong...*man.*

Would my parents even care if I got with a man? I think, as long as it wasn't anyone I was related to, they'd probably be fine with it. Surely.

Unease niggles at me. If they don't, I'll have to listen to endless lectures. Maybe this isn't something I tell them. It can be my little secret.

Logan slowly approaches me until he's so close I can smell him. His scent is different than that of Ryder. Logan smells like freshly brewed coffee with a hint of campfire smoke. I have the urge to step forward so I can bury my face in the crook of his neck, inhaling him until my lungs burn.

We're both quiet as we stare at one another. Logan boldly trails his gaze from my eyes down to my lips. I lick them nervously at having the attention there, which makes him groan. It's a small, quiet sound, but I hear it. My dick certainly hears it, thickening by the second.

"I know what I want," Logan says, voice husky. "And if I took it, I wouldn't want to ever let it go."

His words are more swoonworthy than any of the heroes in the books I read. My knees shake slightly. Every cell in my body aches to be touched by this man. I want his mouth on mine. All over me. Inside me.

Is this what it feels like to fall in love at first sight?

Some of my books—well, at least the ones with sex that Raegan isn't allowed to read—the characters seem to have instant chemistry. While it seemed silly when reading, I'm starting to understand it.

"Who says you'd have to let go?" I reply in a breathless tone.

Logan's eyes darken and he steps impossibly closer. Holy shit. He's going to kiss me. I'm going to get my first kiss from this incredibly hot guy who, by fate, waltzed into my life without warning. I tilt my chin up, desperate for his mouth on mine.

I would give anything for a kiss from him.

Anything.

His nostrils flare as he devours me with his gaze. My eyelids flutter closed, hoping I'm inviting him for the kiss I need. I feel his breath tickle over my face and then—

"Logan!"

Someone calls for him just outside my cabin door, making both of us jolt apart. My face flames with embarrassment.

Logan scowls but then gives me another one of his delicious winks that promises more later. It's enough to keep me from crawling under the bed to hide from all my overwhelming feelings.

Jace comes through the door, eyes quickly darting between us, and then motions for us to follow him. Outside, Rowdy has started a bonfire since the air is growing chillier as the sun sets. Several of our visitors are sitting on the wood benches, warming their hands and faces. The laughter of children by the goat pen can be heard as well. All of it is so…nice. I could get used to all these people who are making my home feel more like a community than ever before.

"Over there," Jace says, pointing to a small woman with jet-black hair. "Shitfaced."

Logan tenses at Jace's words before muttering, "Unbelievable."

The woman sees me staring and rises unsteadily from the bench, a bottle sloshing with liquid as she makes her way toward us. When she's almost to me, she sneers at me. "Kristen. Logan's wife."

It takes a second to process her words.

Wife?

Logan has a wife?

Horror floods through me. Did I really misunderstand all of Logan's actions and words? Was he being friendly but I took it as flirting?

Oh my God.

Logan snatches the bottle from her hand and glowers down at her. "You've had enough. Go to bed."

She opens her mouth like she might say something, but one look at Logan—pissed by the way the vein in his temple jumps—and she decides otherwise.

Logan turns to me, not meeting my eyes. "Sorry," he grumbles. "I need to make sure she gets back to our tent safely."

Our tent.

Fuck.

The sharp, stabbing pain in my chest Logan caused

hurts worse than the constant ache I have for my brother. This pain feels like betrayal. A cruel tease of what I could have but will never get.

Logan looks over his shoulder as he guides his wife away, regret twisting his beautiful mouth into a sad frown. He mouths the words, "I'm sorry," and it's another knife to my chest.

Maybe I didn't imagine things between us.

Maybe he did feel attracted to me.

None of that matters now, though. He's married. Logan Greer has a wife.

And I have no one.

CHAPTER TEN

ryder

DAD CAVED.

For some reason, these people worked their way past his defenses, and now our property is crawling with them. I've never seen so many humans in one place before. Ever. It makes my skin crawl.

What's worse is that both Ronan and Raegan are happy.

Not that I don't want them to be, but I don't trust these newcomers. I'm not like my siblings, and now Dad—ready to throw caution to the wind and accept these people.

Yes, they have lots of women and children.

Yes, that should make me feel safe.

I'm not worried about my own safety, though. I'm worried about my siblings and their feelings. We don't know these people. CJ, from my astute observation, is a massive flirt who just wants to get his dick wet.

In my sister.

The thought is super fucking infuriating.

And this is all happening because Dad let it.

The fire crackles and pops, reminding me I'm supposed to be on watch, not pouting. When Dad went into the big house with Michael and Stacey, the pregnant woman, he silently commanded me and Rowdy to make sure no crazy shit happened without him. Rowdy is doing a better job at keeping an eye on things, hiding in a shadowed part of the yard, leaned up against a tree. I should be watching my younger siblings to make sure they aren't getting into any trouble with the new kids, but I can't scrape the way Raegan looks at CJ from my brain.

Raegan's laughter has me jerking my attention toward the sound. CJ sits beside her, animatedly gesticulating, while both she and Jace crack up. As much as I love her laugh, and it's rare since she's such a crabby bitch most days, I don't want CJ to be the cause of it.

I want to punch him in his stupid smiling face.

If he even thinks about fucking my sister, I'll drag his ass out into the woods and put a major beatdown on him.

Ronan, who has been smiling from ear to ear all evening, now sits on a bench, frowning at his clasped hands. Maybe he's finally seeing through all the bullshit.

I'm about to stand and make my way over to him when CJ's sister plops down beside me. This wouldn't be the first time she's made her interest known. I thought giving her curt, one-worded grunts would be enough to indicate how I feel about her.

Apparently not.

"CJ's a good guy," Mya says, smirking at me. "You don't have to kill him."

"Who says I'm going to kill him?" I grumble.

"Ahh, he speaks!" She cackles and playfully fist pumps the air. "And here I thought you'd gone full caveman. A little civility lives inside the great Ryder Jamison."

I catch Ronan's gaze from over the fire. His frown remains as he darts his eyes back and forth from me to Mya. Giving him a one-shouldered shrug that I hope he interprets as it is—that I don't know how to get rid of this annoying girl—I turn to give Mya a flat stare.

"Don't you have someone else to bother?"

"Nope."

"Isn't it past your bedtime?"

"Ha."

"Seriously, I'm not in the mood."

She sighs and pats my thigh. "*Teenage Angst in the Wilderness*. Sounds like a book title." Her grin turns wicked. "Oh, wait? Can cavemen read?"

I scowl at her, knocking her hand off my leg. "Fuck off."

"And if I don't?" she teases. "Going to club me and drag me by my hair back to your cave?" She lets out a snort and then whispers, "Don't worry. I'm a kinky bitch."

Scrubbing my palm over my face, I ignore her, letting my eyes find my brother again. He's staring at the open gate, a gut-wrenching look of loneliness marring his features.

"Have fun talking to yourself," I grumble as I rise to my feet. "Not interested."

Mya huffs and mutters, "Asshole."

She's barking up the wrong tree if she thinks I want to spend more than five minutes with her. I don't like any of these people or the fact they're infiltrating our property like fire ants.

I step over a woman curled up on a blanket with a toddler tucked at her side and then sit beside Ronan. His tense body relaxes at my proximity, making me feel a whole lot better. Slinging my arm over his shoulders, I hug him to me. He smells like fruit with a hint of cinnamon. Always has for some reason. His scent is comforting.

"These people are fucking dicks," I complain. "Mya called me a caveman."

Ronan doesn't wriggle free of my affection, instead slumping against me. It makes me want to pull him closer, reminding all these damn trespassers that he's my brother, not their new source of entertainment.

"You kind of are a caveman. You have a wolf for a pet."

I snort out a laugh, my gaze darting over to Raegan, who has Mage wrapped up in a blanket in her arms like he's a baby and not some wild animal. "Ex pet. He's a traitor."

Ronan trembles and I wonder if he's cold. I squeeze his shoulder and then rub up and down to bring warmth to his flesh.

"Are we good?" I ask, unable to stop the cracking of my voice. "I feel like these people took you guys away from me."

Ronan looks up at me, eyes burning hot like the fire behind his glasses. "Of course we're good. I'm right here where I belong."

His words soothe my heart that'd been feeling bruised and abused. "Yeah?"

"Yeah."

"Hopefully these assholes will be gone soon."

"Hope so too," he says sadly. "Raegan won't like it, though."

"Rae has us. She doesn't need those fuckers."

One of said fuckers whispers something to her and she howls with laughter. Yep, I want to kill them both, especially CJ.

"Where'd Logan go?" I ask, forcing my attention back to my brother.

He shudders—again, I think from the cold, but am beginning to wonder. "His wife."

The venomous way with which he utters those words confuses me. Why does he seem mad that Logan has a wife? A sudden thought occurs to me, but I shove it away.

Nah.

Not Ronan.

I've seen all the porn mags Wild smuggles him and they're all women.

"Logan seems like an even bigger dick than his brother and cousin," I state with a shrug. "I'm your friend. Fuck them."

Ronan's lips twitch on one corner with an almost smile. "Yeah, I guess you're right."

"I know I'm right."

Dad, with Michael on his tail, returns to the bonfire. He motions for Rowdy, who materializes from the darkness to join us.

"Bad news is she's having contractions," Dad tells us. "Good news is, they're most likely Braxton Hicks, and she just needs rest. Your momma is setting her up in the girls' room." He turns his eyes to me. "I trust you can keep an eye on Destiny and Raegan since they'll be staying next door for a few days?"

Ronan groans under his breath. I'd be annoyed too if I had to give up my cabin for the girls. But everything about these people is annoying and invasive. It's no surprise they're taking over the house too.

"I'll watch them," I say in agreement. "Me and Ronan both will."

Ronan nods, though I can tell he's still butt hurt about giving up his cabin. Michael shoots us a grateful smile for readjusting our lives to accommodate his family. Whatever, man. This isn't about pleasing him.

It's about respecting Dad's wishes and protecting my own family.

Now that Dad is back and everything seems to be back under control, I rise to my feet and holler at Rae. "Bedtime, brat. You too, Dez."

Raegan tries to complain, but one scathing glare from Dad and she bites back her words. She glowers at me like she has the power to intimidate me. She doesn't.

While me and Ronan gather up our sisters, I avoid Mya altogether. She's fucking weird and I don't have any plans to spend another second near her. We're almost to the cabins when I feel another presence. Glancing over my shoulder, I notice Rowdy trailing behind.

Ronan goes inside his cabin, most likely to grab his things, and the girls trail after. I stop to give Rowdy an assessing look.

"What are your plans?" I ask, crossing my arms over my chest.

He shrugs. "Probably sleep on your hammock if you have an extra blanket. If not, Spirit can keep me warm. Not going back to my place anytime soon."

Not because of the momma bear and her cubs.

Nah, he's here to keep watch just as I am.

"Think we should take turns walking the perimeter tonight?"

He nods, scooping up Spirit and nuzzling the wolf pup's fur with his nose. "I'd feel safer if we did."

"Me too." I stifle a yawn. "You want first watch?"

My older brother smirks. "Yeah. Get your beauty sleep, princess."

I'm stunned for a moment as I realize Rowdy is teasing me. Like old times. Like before he went on his fateful trip. Maybe he's on the road to recovery. It'd be great to see him laugh again.

I flip him off but then abandon him to go into my cabin. I briefly see Raegan dart in to steal Mage's food and water bowls, before she disappears again. Her and Ronan's muffled voices can be heard outside and then a few minutes later, he joins me in my cabin.

Normally, I don't mind being alone, but tonight I'm glad to have my brother with me. I start the fire in my fireplace and then shed all my clothes down to my boxers. Ronan is being fucking weird, staring a hole into the ground.

"Dude," I say with a laugh. "You can't sleep in your boots."

Giving my back to him, I crawl into my bed, taking the spot by the wall. Soon, I can hear soft thuds as he removes his boots and clothes. He still won't look at me as he slides into bed, which makes my chest squeeze painfully.

Something's wrong with Ronan.

"You know you can talk to me," I murmur, propping my body up on one elbow so I can look at him. "You don't have to suffer in silence."

Ronan's lips thin out as if he's trying to hold words inside his mouth. I want to pry them open with my fingers, freeing them for me to consume greedily. Playfully, I tug at his bottom lip with my fingers.

"Tell me," I order, grinning at him.

He smiles back and then bites my finger. Fucker. I howl in exaggerated pain that has us both cracking up. When we settle down, he's no longer being strange and smiles happily at me. My heart hammers in my chest with pride. I'm thankful I can make him feel better.

Since he doesn't seem keen on speaking, I stretch out beside him, resting my head on the pillow beside his. He doesn't push me away when I drape an arm over him. Something tells me he needs to feel like he's loved and a part of this family. That's something I can endlessly give him.

He's my brother.

My best friend.

Mine.

Those fuckers—Logan and CJ and Jace—don't get to steal my people from me.

Ronan sucks in a sharp breath when my fingers dance over his lower abs. He's always been ticklish. I'm not going to terrorize him by pinning him down, but gently tickling him and listening to his breath hitch is amusing. Again, he doesn't stop me.

"Do you ever feel like you want something you're not allowed to have?" he asks, voice barely a whisper.

I think about Raegan. Beautiful and sassy and arousing and fucking off-limits.

"Maybe," I say, allowing a little of my truth to bleed into the word.

Is he being weird because he really does like Logan, but he's married?

"It's okay to like a man." My words are hot against the side of his face. "You know that, right?"

He makes a keening sound, swiftly flipping onto his side and giving me his back, no doubt trying to hide from me what I've guessed. That he likes Logan. Not letting him escape that easily, I curl around him, nuzzling his hair with my nose.

Loved and accepted.

That's what I want him to feel.

"You can have that one day," I promise, "just not with him."

"Not with who?" he croaks out, playing dumb.

"Logan. I see how you look at him. Like you're in love."

"I'm not in love with some guy I just met," he grumbles in a defensive tone. "You don't know everything, Ry."

I kiss his shoulder, again in an effort to make him feel loved and accepted, before whispering, "Good to know. You deserve someone better than Logan."

"And who would that be, oh wise one?" he prods. "Who, Ry? Look around us. There's no one like me. I'm all alone."

Irritated by his words, I hug him closer. My body flickers with heat and I wonder if I made the fire too hot. The smart thing would be to stop cuddling Ronan so I don't sweat my ass off, but I can't find it in me to let go.

"You'll never be alone," I murmur. "You'll always have me."

"Are you volunteering yourself to get fucked?"

I snort out a laugh and playfully tease, "Maybe *I'd* be the one doing all the fucking." To punctuate my words, I push my dick against his ass.

He elbows me hard in the gut. "I hate you. You're such a dick sometimes."

"Love you too, big bro."

I drift off with a smile on my face. Our joking around about being lovers has put us both in a better mood. His soft breathing indicates he finally succumbed to sleep.

Ronan will find someone worthy one day.

Someone he can fuck since he's clearly horrified by the idea of taking it.

And I will support him one hundred percent.

As long as it's not Logan or any of those trespassers.

I'd volunteer myself if that meant saving him from that skeevy guy. My traitorous dick pressed against Ronan's ass plumps, turning to stone as images of me being the one to bring him pleasure invade my mind.

Thank fuck he's asleep because there'd be no way to explain my way out of that shit.

Maybe my dick really is broken since I can't seem to keep it under control around Raegan and now Ronan.

Teenage Angst in the Wilderness sounds like a stupid book.

One star.

Do not recommend.

CHAPTER ELEVEN

raegan

They've been here five days and Dad still hasn't kicked them out. It's a miracle, really. Especially since Dad hates everyone.

But he doesn't hate them.

He and Mom have also been too busy to harp on me and my brothers about the creek incident. I was sure I was going to get an ass whipping for all that mouthing off I did.

It never came.

Maybe my parents could see I wasn't being unreasonable. I don't like Wild and have no plans to marry that freak.

For the past few days, I've managed to get CJ alone several times, dragging him past the food jungle along the fence where we're hidden. Despite his teasing and charm, he's actually well-behaved and hasn't so much as tried to kiss me. It's driving me insane.

"I don't like them," Destiny says from where she's curled up on Ronan's bed in my usual spot.

Not that I'm complaining. I took over his spot and inhaled his cinnamon-scented pillow every night like a lovesick stalker.

"Who?" I ask, playing dumb. "Kota and Declan?"

She sighs like a girl much older than fourteen. "No. The trespassers."

I want to punch Ryder for making that title stick. That's what everyone besides me and Ronan refers to them as.

"Why not?" I huff from the floor where I'm watching Mage slurp up water from his bowl. "They're nice. Don't be a snob, Dez."

She combs her bony fingers through her pale blond hair, frowning at me. Though I'm probably no more than a blob of shadow to her, she pins me with a penetrating stare that makes my skin feel itchy.

"I'm not a snob," she says patiently, ignoring my agitated squirming. "I just don't trust them."

"Because they're nice?" I snap. "You're just used to Dad and Rowdy and Ryder. Not everyone is a paranoid asshole."

She flinches at my harsh words. "Just be careful around them, okay?"

"Maybe if you'd actually try to get to know them, you wouldn't act like that. Have you even attempted to speak to Mya?" I demand. "What about Jace or CJ or any of the other kids close to our ages?"

Guilt makes my sister bow her head. I feel like a witch biting her head off, but she's not even giving them a chance.

"I guess not," she allows. "You're right. I can try harder. It's just always been us and the Knox family. These other people make me nervous."

I toss a stick at Mage, but he ignores it in favor of gnawing on my boot. His sister, Spirit, is the better of the two wolf pups and doesn't chew on everything under the sun, which is why Dad's been letting her go into the big house. Mage would probably chew my little brothers to bits. Not that they wouldn't deserve it.

A hard knock on the door makes both me and Destiny squeak in surprise. Mage stops chewing to yap at the sound.

I bound to my feet and rush over to answer it, expecting Ronan to be dropping by for more clothes or something. My disappointment at not seeing him is brief, followed by excitement at seeing CJ instead.

"Want to go on an adventure today?" CJ asks, flashing me a brilliant, flirty grin that makes my insides twist.

"Absolutely," I chirp. "Let me put on my boots and grab my knife."

It'll always be my knife. Just like Mage is my pup. Ryder will have to get over these things.

"Jace has booze," CJ reveals as Jace waggles his brows at me. "Carter over there has candy and beef jerky."

Carter, one of the other kids I haven't met before, stands awkwardly behind them but nods in agreement. He's fifteen or sixteen if I had to guess, though he doesn't look like Jace or CJ with their red hair, green eyes, and freckles. Carter is thin, blue-eyed, and has shaggy black hair. He definitely must be a part of one of the other families that's in their group.

"Destiny loves candy and beef jerky," I say, hinting at my sister that this is her moment to get to know them. "Right, sis?"

She nods slowly. "Yeah, but I don't want to hold you all back on your adventure."

Jace saunters into the room and plops down on the bed beside my sister. Her cheeks burn bright red. I have to stifle a snort of amusement.

"We'll keep you safe, Destiny," Jace assures her. "You can hold my hand if you need to."

It's sweet of him to want to help my nearly blind sister. CJ slings an arm over my shoulders, tugging me to him.

"It's settled," CJ says in triumph. "Let's get out of here before any parents notice. I'm so not doing chores today."

"Fuck chores," Jace agrees, playfully nudging Destiny.

"I do hate chores," Dez blurts out and then giggles.

Ten minutes later and we're all slipping past the adults standing around the fire and hurrying out of the gate. The tents from CJ's group are scattered around the woods. Crying babies, soft singing, and occasional voices can be heard. Not all of the people are as friendly as CJ and Jace. Most still seem skittish, hanging back in their tents and letting Michael and Owen do all the entertaining.

When we reach the end of the fence, I make sure Jace is doing as promised—holding Destiny's hand—before trotting ahead to take the lead. Mage bounces after me, darting through CJ's feet and nearly making him fall on his face. We all quietly laugh at his near misfortune. Eventually, we make it around the back side of our fortified property to the steps that will take us down the cliffside to the river. Long ago, probably before I was born, Dad and Uncle Atticus built the stairs to make it easier for us to get water when we didn't have a rainwater collection system in place yet.

"Be careful," I warn everyone behind me. "One misstep and you'll take quite a tumble. I still have a scar on my knee from falling once. A wrong move and you could break your neck."

I look over my shoulder to see if anyone is intimidated by my words. Carter is frowning and appears to be slightly afraid. CJ is grinning from ear to ear, which is his usual MO. Jace and Destiny both wear determined expressions as they carefully make their way down.

Maybe I'll scare them about bears instead.

"Rowdy says there's a momma grizzly around here and she's territorial over her cubs," I tell them when I reach the bottom of the steps, slightly out of breath. "Who will she eat first?"

This earns me a better reaction. All four of my adventure mates frown at me. Satisfied, I smirk and continue along the path toward Rowdy's house. Not that he's there. He's been stalking us and the property, doing Dad's bidding to protect us.

CJ sidles up next to me, taking hold of my hand. At first, I think he's afraid of my bear talk, but then his thumb strokes over my flesh, sending goose bumps over my skin. I cut my eyes his way, unable to keep my heart from tripping over itself when he flashes me a wicked smile.

We are holding hands.

Oh my God.

I know my face is hot, but I don't even care. I'm holding hands with a cute guy who is very much into me. Best part is that I don't think my parents care. As long as I don't have sex with my brothers, they're good.

Jace chatters to Destiny, explaining things as we walk, while I get caught up in a fantasy of me and CJ. Alone and naked. Him on top of me, his penis hard and ready.

Like Ryder's cock.

But smaller because the more I think about Ryder's cock, the more I decide it's too big to be going anywhere near my vagina.

Maybe CJ has a finger-sized penis. My finger fits inside me just fine.

The more I think about sexual stuff, the more flustered I get. I should have grabbed a canteen of water so I could dump it over my head right about now.

Our hike takes us past Rowdy's cabin that my parents lived in a long time ago and onto a piece of land where Aunt Eve used to live. There supposedly used to be a shack there, but Uncle Atticus and Dad leveled it way before my memories go.

Jace stops and gives Carter a playful shove. "Snacks, bro. We're hungry."

CJ tugs me over to a fallen log and I sit down beside him on it. I suppress a shiver when his arm snakes around my waist, his large hand settling on my hip. Jace guides Destiny to a soft pile of pine straw and then starts unzipping Carter's backpack. He passes out some bottles of water and then the snacks. I guess the promised booze is for later, not that I'm complaining.

"I love Skittles!" I exclaim, snatching the red bag out of Jace's hands. "They're my favorites."

Jace chuckles. "Didn't know you people would even know what they were."

"We live in the wilderness, but we're not uncivilized, dork." I happily rip open my bag and dump a bunch of candies into my mouth. The sweetness is an instant joyful high.

Carter stands aside, arms hanging at his sides and not saying a word. What a weird kid. If I'd met him instead of CJ and Jace, I'd have definitely run in the other direction. Jace, upon seeing me watch Carter, smirks my way before grabbing Carter's shoulders.

"Sit, Cart. You're making everyone nervous." He pushes down on Carter so that he's forced to sit down on the pine needles next to my sister. "There. Better. Don't get handsy with little Destiny or I'll have to punch you."

Carter swallows hard and brings his knees to his chest in an effort to stay away from Destiny. Good. I don't want that freak touching her because then I would have to punch him too.

We stay long enough to finish our water bottles and snacks. Skittles and beef jerky—the store-bought kind, not the homemade kind—wrappers flutter across the earth. I feel like we should probably pick them up, because if Dad were here he would make us, but then think better of it. I'm not going to be the bossy mom on our adventure today.

"Think I can heave this rock all the way into the river?" Jace asks, a round stone in his hand. "CJ, come on, let's bet."

CJ shakes his head. "You used to play baseball. Not falling for it."

Jace, not one to be stopped, rears back his arm and then sends the rock sailing. It hits one of the trees near the river with a loud *thunk* and then goes straight down.

I bark out a laugh and then nudge CJ. "Should have taken the bet!"

CJ grumbles but picks up a different stone. He throws his, but it doesn't go quite as far. Jace is about to throw another one when he looks at the rock, brows scrunching together.

"Who names rocks in the middle of the fucking forest?" With a shrug, he throws the one in his hand, this one making a splash in the river.

My blood runs cold at his words. I whirl around and notice the rocks they've been throwing—and continue to throw—are those of a grave. Or several graves to be exact.

"No!" I cry out, smacking a rock out of CJ's hand. "Stop! You have to go get them. Right now!"

CJ frowns in confusion. "What? Why?"

"My aunt," I blurt, "lost several babies. Those are their graves."

CJ's eyes widen in horror and Jace frowns like he might be sick. Guilt has my stomach twisting painfully. I may hate Wild, but his mother is awesome. I love Aunt Eve. Knowing we disturbed the grave of her many unborn children makes me want to throw up.

"Hey," CJ says, clutching my wrist gently. "It's okay. We'll get them and put them back. We didn't know."

I nod, swallowing hard. I catch Destiny also frowning, her bottom lip wobbling. Carter doesn't say a word, just tries to stay out of the way.

Something moving behind a tree has me stalling in my effort to collect the rocks that were thrown. The hairs on my arms stand on end. It's the growl—deep and threatening—that makes me completely freeze up.

Bear.

"Shit," Jace hisses. "Is that a fucking bear?"

I whimper and give him the briefest of nods. To my absolute horror, Destiny is the closest to the bear that's standing on its hind legs to appear more menacing.

And it's a huge female grizzly—at least seven feet tall and around four hundred pounds if I had to guess. Destiny is dwarfed by the beast's massive stature.

"I'm scared," Destiny cries out and then takes off running.

As she blindly darts past me and slams her shoulder into a tree that sends her flopping to the forest floor, the angry bear begins its chase. Mage howls, scampering off into the trees, away from the predator. All I can do is stare at the grizzly as it rushes us, snarling and growling in fury. It rises up on its two hind legs again when it's near and then swipes at the person closest to it.

Carter.

The kid goes flying, the bear's claws shredding through his backpack and emptying the contents in one fell swoop. Still, I can't move my feet, and from the looks of it, neither can Jace or CJ.

We're all going to die.

Grab your knife, dummy!

My knife, sheathed at my belt, remains untouched because I can't move.

The bear sinks its teeth into the back of Carter's leg, making him scream in pain. The bear stands on its two hind legs once more, drawing Carter off the ground, letting him dangle by where it has him captured in its jaws.

We have to do something!

Boom!

The echoing sound of gunfire has me crying out in surprise. The bear makes a pained sound, dropping Carter to the ground before turning around.

Boom! Boom! Boom! Boom!

With each shot, the bear jerks, but it's the one to its face that ultimately sends it crashing to the ground. Then, more shots ring out.

Someone is screaming.

Me. It's me. I'm screaming.

The scene begins to clear around me. One big bear is dead. Several small ones up ahead are now dead too. And Rowdy emerges, holstering his .45, wearing a murderous expression. His hair having come loose from his man bun and overgrown beard make him look like a predator too, but this one loves us and just killed these animals to protect us.

I know we'll be in trouble for this, but I can't find it in me to care right now. Snatching Destiny's hand, I jerk her up and we both run right into our oldest brother's waiting arms. We both sob uncontrollably, letting him assure us that everything's all better now that the bears are dead.

Our crying calms down, but that's when I realize someone else is crying.

Carter.

Crap.

"He's hurt," I choke out, pulling away from Rowdy. "The bear bit him."

Jace and CJ are kneeling beside Carter, one holding his hand and speaking in soothing tones while the other is trying to apply a tourniquet to his thigh.

This is bad.

This is so bad.

CHAPTER TWELVE

ronan

PAINED SCREAMS PIERCE THE AIR, MAKING everyone around the campfire look up from their bowls of oatmeal in confusion.

I latch eyes with Dad for about two seconds and then I realize he's counting children. When he comes up short, he takes off out of the yard in a full sprint.

Several moments later, chaos ensues as Dad returns with my sisters and Mage, Jace, CJ, and some other kid in Rowdy's arms.

There's blood everywhere.

I snap into action about the same time Ryder does, both of us running toward our siblings in an effort to make sure they're okay. First thing I notice is both Destiny and Raegan have been bawling—red-faced and snotty-nosed.

"Take care of your sisters," Dad barks out at me and Ryder.

An entourage of people go into the house no doubt

to deal with the bleeding boy. When Raegan sees me, she crumples, a loud sob escaping her. Ryder hugs Destiny to him since she's closer and I grab Raegan. Raegan clings to me, soaking my shirt as she cries into my neck.

"What happened?" I ask, gently stroking her back. "Rae, what happened?"

Through her hiccupping and tears, I hear the word, "bears," and it's enough for me to figure out what happened. They were attacked and the kid got mauled. Better him than my sisters. I catch Ryder's worried stare and he silently gestures for me to go sit at the firepit. We lead the girls to the end of one of the long C-shaped benches, sandwiching them between us.

As Rae regains her composure, she recounts what happened from the moment they left until now. I'd thought they were doing chores or sleeping in. I never saw them leave the property. Based on Ryder's same guilty expression, he feels just as terrible as I do for letting this happen under our watch.

I notice we've drawn a crowd of people. Mya kneels on the gravel near Ryder, a concerned frown on her face as she listens.

"Is my brother okay?" Mya asks. "He and Jace went into the big house with all of our dads and Carter. I'm worried."

Rae nods. "They're fine. It was just Carter who got hurt."

"What were you all thinking?" Mya demands,

concern melting away as anger storms its way in. "There's a reason why we have a big group. Safety in numbers. It's too dangerous to sneak off just so you can suck my brother's dick!"

Rae recoils at her nasty words. "You're one to talk. I see how you look at *my* brother."

Several people whisper and someone barks out an inappropriate laugh. I hug Rae closer and whisper for her to quit. Of course she ignores me. That's my sister for you.

"He doesn't want you and yet you still try," Rae continues, voice quavering. "Get over it. You look desperate."

"Bitch," Mya snarls, rising to her feet and then storming off.

Ryder shakes his head in disbelief. What a shit show.

"What'd I miss?" CJ asks as he walks over to us, Jace on his heels.

I glance over his blood-splattered shirt and shudder. "Nothing worth repeating."

Raegan tugs out of my hold and rushes over to CJ. He collects her in his arms and barely spares us another look before guiding her away from the crowd around the fire. Jace remains, his stare on my other sister lingering a little longer than I feel comfortable with.

"Let's go," I tell Ryder and gesture for Destiny. "She needs to get away from all these people."

Especially these bad influences.

Ryder nods and then scoops Destiny into his arms

as he stands. Jace takes a step forward, like he might go with us, but freezes when he meets my nasty warning glare.

I follow my brother to my cabin and then help her get settled. She curls up under the blanket and cries quietly. I'm sure this morning must've been traumatizing for them all.

"I'm going to check on Rae," Ryder says after a few minutes. "Keep an eye on Dez."

Sitting with my sister does nothing to quiet the raging thoughts in my mind. I'd been so eager to have people join us, but they've been nothing but stress and trouble since they arrived. I'm beginning to understand why Dad was so angry with us for bringing them around. Things were quieter and safer without them.

As if to punctuate my thoughts, I hear Ryder yelling just outside the cabin. I leave Destiny to see what the hell is going on, nearly tripping over Mage, who rushes into the cabin. Outside, I find Ryder shoving CJ.

"Hey," I call out to my brother. "What's the problem?"

Raegan stands in front of CJ and glowers at Ryder. "I can kiss whomever I want."

"The fuck you can," Ryder growls, baring his teeth. "He touches you again and I'll kill him."

I can tell Raegan is about to punch Ryder, so I rush over to them to prevent them from brawling. Grabbing Ryder by the back of the shirt, I drag him a few feet away from our feisty sister.

"Enough," I tell them both. "Everyone is upset after what happened. You all need to calm down."

"No," Rae hisses at me. "CJ and I went through a traumatic event together. He kissed me and it felt nice. Comforting. I don't need Ryder making a big deal out of it!"

Ryder starts forward, but my grip on his shirt prevents him from getting far. "Why did you kiss him? You barely know him!"

This is getting out of hand. Fast.

"You should leave," I warn CJ. "Now."

CJ's brow deepens as determination sets in.

"If you stay, we'll both kick your ass," I snap. "Go the fuck away."

So much for being the peacekeeper.

Raegan turns her nasty glare on me. "Traitor."

CJ wisely storms off, but not without promising to find Raegan later. That comment makes Ryder bristle with rage.

When I'm sure my siblings won't murder each other, I motion for them to both follow me. The hammock in front of Ryder's cabin is empty, but the blanket Rowdy was using remains draped over it. I somehow manage to get both Ryder and Raegan to sit with me on the hammock, me being the lucky one to get squashed in the middle.

I try to ignore the warmth of Ryder's thigh burning hot against my own. A few nights ago he'd sent confusing messages my way. It was as if he was flirting with me, which is insane because it's impossible. And because it was probably another mistake on my part like with my wishful thinking and Logan, it never happened again. A blissful moment gone all too soon.

It was a fading memory until now, feeling his hot touch.

"This isn't us," I say softly, grabbing both of their hands. "We don't fight like this."

Both of my siblings snort.

"Maybe not you," Raegan says with amusement, "but this is sort of our thing, me and Ryder."

"Fighting about stupid shit," I agree. "But not letting other people come between you."

They're both quiet for a bit. Just the three of us, silent and relaxing, reminds me of times beyond this past week. We're best friends. Bickering is normal, but this great divide between us is not.

"I still don't understand what the big deal is," Raegan says softly. "It was just a kiss. I like him. You guys know I like him. I thought you two of all people would want me to be happy."

Ryder bristles but manages not to growl when he replies. "It's not you who's the problem here, Rae. It's him. He's bad news. Just look how today turned out."

"It's not his fault we were attacked by a bear," she mutters. "We live in the wild. It's a part of life here."

"It is his fault that he took you away from us and our protection. If I were there," Ryder grinds out, "I could have protected you and Dez. Did CJ even bring a weapon? He's fucking clueless."

"Rowdy was stalking us. Don't worry." She shoots Ryder a scathing glare. "Crisis averted."

This is getting nowhere.

"Look," I say to Raegan. "We get it. It sucks sometimes being out here away from people. We don't get to experience the same things everyone else does."

She nods emphatically in agreement, so I continue.

"But it doesn't mean you have to jump the first guy you meet." I arch a brow at her. "He's not even that cute."

Ryder smothers a laugh. Based on the confused expression Raegan's wearing, I know I'll have to explain.

"I, uh," I stammer, rocking the hammock a little too hard that we all have to lean forward to keep from being dumped out. "I just…I know when a guy looks good or not."

Raegan gasps comically. "Ro! Do you like… Are you…"

"I just know," I spit out in exasperation. "There's lots I don't know, but I can tell you CJ is just average. I mean, I know you hate him, but have you seen Wild?"

She cackles so hard she nearly topples us again. "Oh my God! You think Wild is hot? This is too good! Maybe you can marry him and I'll finally be off the hook!"

"Then maybe you can stop scraping the bottom of the barrel since you won't feel like you're out of options," Ryder suggests with a grunt. "For the record, I wouldn't wish Wild on anyone in this family."

"He's not that bad," I argue as Raegan says, "Right?!"

He really isn't that bad. Arrogant and bossy as fuck. A little bit of a psychopath when he wants to be. But because he's hot, just as Raegan said, I can forgive him for those things.

"We're going to be okay," I assure them both, ignoring their jabbing at Wild. "Right?"

Ryder nods, smirking at me. "We always are."

Raegan leans up against me, sighing. "Yup."

"If you need to practice kissing, Fleabag could be up for the job." Ryder snorts at his dumb idea.

Raegan practically leaps across me to sock him in the shoulder. The move is enough that we all flip in the hammock, landing in a painful heap on the wooden porch, howls of laughter following.

Things are back to normal all right. We spend the rest of the day cracking jokes and bonding. Ryder even pulls out his acoustic guitar to play a few songs, including a silly one about Raegan he makes up words to.

I'm grinning at Ryder when Logan rushes around the corner, panting and eyes frantic. Immediately the hairs on my arms stand on end. The three of us scramble to our feet.

"What is it?" I demand, not entirely sure I want to know the answer.

"It's…" he chokes out, terror twisting his features. "My wife. Kristen. She's gone."

"What do you mean gone?" I step forward, the

urge to calm him overwhelming. "Maybe she just took a walk."

He violently shakes his head. "N-No. When I went into the tent just now to check on her, there was blood."

"Bear?" Raegan croaks, voice quivering.

"I don't know," Logan hisses. "Fuck. I don't know where she is, but I have a really bad feeling about this."

I step away from my siblings to grab onto his biceps and meet his panicked stare. "We'll help you look for her. It's okay. We'll figure this out together."

He rapidly nods before pulling me to him in a crushing hug. Days ago I might have died to have this moment with him. Knowing what I know now, that he has a wife, I'm not as comfortable with this hug. Still, I'm not an asshole and give him the comfort he so clearly needs.

"Help me find her, please," Logan begs, breath hot against my neck. "We were trying to get pregnant and she recently missed her period. What if we were finally going to have a baby only for something horrible to happen to them both?"

He shudders in my arms. It explains why he was so pissed she was drinking the other day. Whenever my mom has been pregnant in the past, she avoided alcohol because it was bad for the unborn child.

"We'll find her. She's going to be okay," I lie, rubbing my palms up and down his back. "I promise."

Ryder steps into my view and I don't miss the

annoyed look he gives Logan. I know he doesn't like him, but now's not the time for any of that.

We have to find Kristen.

Because, whether it's a predator who took her from where she slept or she wandered off after drinking too much, it won't matter. The wilderness is dangerous. And not everyone who dares to enter it will survive it.

CHAPTER THIRTEEN

ryder

LOGAN NEEDS TO STOP TOUCHING MY BROTHER. What is it about these people infiltrating our land and then putting their grubby paws all over my siblings? It's weird and it's gross and I want them to fucking stop.

I clear my throat, reminding Logan his wife is missing and maybe just maybe he needs to stop hugging Ronan so we can go find her.

They finally break apart, but I don't miss how Logan lingers in close proximity to Ronan, nor do I miss the pink stain on Ronan's cheeks.

Irritation has me grunting and gesturing for Logan to lead the way. Once he passes, Ronan steps beside me, and much to my annoyance, so does Rae.

"Go sit with Dez," I growl to her.

She huffs, lifting her chin high, and hisses back, "You go sit with Dez. I'm going out there to look for Kristen and you can't stop me."

Unbelievable.

Our group makes it out the gate and then we traipse through the trees until we find a smattering of tents set up. Logan takes us over to one of the bigger ones and unzips it before stepping aside. I crouch down in front of the opening and peer inside.

Like he said, there's blood and it's smeared on the blankets that are rumpled and shoved away too as though the person fought their attacker. There aren't any signs of damage to the outside of the tent, which leads me to believe this was not a bear.

"Anyone from your camp missing?" I ask once I stand back up.

Raegan, unable to resist, also peeks inside. "Not a bear," she concludes after a few seconds. "This place would be smashed and shredded if so."

No one calls her Captain Obvious, though it's on the tip of my tongue. Luckily, Logan responds before I can lash her with my barb.

"All present and accounted for." He scrubs a palm over his face and shoots me a harrowing look. "I honestly worried it was you who'd taken her."

I stiffen at his words. "Me?"

He shrugs as though it's a no-brainer. I'm left reeling, and quite frankly, offended.

"Why Ryder?" Ronan asks, a frown tugging at his pouty lips.

"We barely know you all," Logan says with a huff.

"No offense to you, personally, but you weren't with the group that got attacked by the bear."

"Neither was I," Ronan offers.

"I know it wasn't you." Logan's smile is small and private for Ronan, but I still see.

"We won't find her sitting around with our thumbs up our asses," I grunt, shooting Logan a warning glare. "We need to gather some capable hands and then divide our groups up to cover more ground."

Logan hesitates, as if my assuming command grates on him, but he manages to swallow down his ire, giving me a quick nod.

It's dark by the time we have a group of twelve organized and ready to go on our hunt. Logan makes sure Ronan is in his group along with his brother Jace. I'm not happy, but I know he can handle himself. I grab Raegan and another man—Michael and Owen's cousin, I learn—named Tom. The other two groups are led by CJ and another one of their cousins and Tom's brother, Seth. Raegan is the only female—another reason why it's best she's in my group.

Once we're all armed and dressed for hunting, another quick ten minutes later, we all set out in different directions. Seth's group goes down the side of the cliff on the stairs to scout out the area along the river, CJ's group goes down the road that leads toward town, my group heads west into an area where we hunt a lot, and Logan's group starts off toward the creek and where we first met up with them.

Normally, Raegan would be running her mouth right about now, still chastising me about earlier, but she's in huntress mode. Her knife—*my* knife—is in her hand and at the ready. Each step she makes is damn near silent and a stark comparison to the way Tom bulldozes his way through the forest, shining his flashlight all over the place with no rhyme or reason.

I want to tell this dude to quit fucking stomping, but I manage to hold myself back. Tom may seem like a doofus, but he's hulking at nearly six and a half feet tall, reminding me very much of Uncle Atticus in size. Dad taught us from an early age not to go provoking creatures that are bigger than us. Tom, though a little pudgy in the midsection, could probably lob my head off with one swing.

My mind is still scattered, thinking about Logan and Ronan and now Tom the giant, when Rae sucks in a sharp breath. It takes only seconds to discover what has her alarmed.

A sock.

Slowly, with my heart beginning to hammer in my chest, I crouch to pick it up, inspecting it closer with my flashlight. A single drop of blood stains the dingy cotton bright crimson. It's dry, which can't be good.

"Kristen's?" Rae asks, picking it up to inspect it better.

It's just a sock and could essentially be anyone's, but not just anyone is missing. Kristen is missing and we've just found our first clue.

"I think we're headed in the right direction," Tom rumbles, worry tinging his tone.

"Stay aware and keep your weapons ready," I remind them both. "If something attacked her, like a mountain lion or something, it's possible it could have dragged her out here. And if we're encroaching on its meal, the cat won't be happy. Shoot first, ask questions later."

Dad would be proud of that last sentiment that has Tom studying me with narrowed eyes.

Ignoring him, I take the lead once more, taking care not to make too much sound. Thankfully, Tom seems to have gotten the hint and isn't smashing his massive boots through anything and everything. Raegan prowls much like a cat herself, making my heart squeeze with momentary pride. As much as I don't want her traipsing out headfirst into danger, I know she of all people can handle herself.

We spend another twenty minutes in silence, the three of us wary and watchful. It's not until Rae sucks in a sharp breath do my eyes also latch onto what she sees.

Blue jeans.

Or, rather, blood-soaked blue jeans sliced cleanly up each pant leg and discarded like trash. My stomach clenches like a fist and bile burns in the back of my throat. No forest animal that I know of can cut neatly through fabric.

Whoever did this is human.

Tom curses under his breath and then stomps past us to inspect the clothing. I'm still wondering who the fuck could do this when Rae cries out and then takes off in a full sprint ahead. It takes a second for my mind to catch up before I'm tearing off after her bouncing flashlight. If the monster who did this is still out here, then she's in danger. We're all in danger.

I've nearly caught up to Rae, weaving around thick tree trunks and hopping over thick underbrush when I see her. Not Rae. Kristen.

Bloody. Half-naked. Unmoving.

Is she dead?

Her legs are crudely spread apart, her pussy on full display, with her underwear still hanging on to one of her legs just past her knee. It's nothing like the dirty magazines Wild smuggles to us. There's nothing sexy about seeing a real pussy for the first time.

This is disgusting.

Kristen is battered with bruises and cuts all over her body. Her face is nearly unrecognizable as it's so purple and swollen. Her bottom lip is split and easily the size of a small plum. Both eyes are hidden from the swelling, making it difficult to tell if she's alive or not.

Rae falls to her knees beside the ruined woman, a soft keening sound escaping my sister. I don't know what to do except stare in horror. When Tom finally arrives, he lets out a pained sound that doesn't sound too far off from the sound Rae made.

"G-Go get help," I order, my voice a raspy croak. "Tom, go. Run."

He hesitates for a second and then takes off, crashing through the forest like a damn crazed grizzly bear.

Rae gently takes hold of Kristen's knee and pushes it toward the other one, eliminating the gruesome, crude evidence of what happened.

Someone raped her and then killed her.

A pained moan resounds from in front of me, finally snapping me into action.

"She's alive," I choke out, falling to my knees on Kristen's other side. "Fuck, what do we do?"

Rae takes Kristen's bloody hand and leans forward. "Kristen, we're here. You're safe now. We'll protect you."

Kristen moans, her agony apparent in the way she shudders and tears roll down her abused cheeks. It kills me seeing this woman like this. Who could do such a fucked-up thing? Someone from the camp? Someone else out there?

"Who hurt you?" I demand, unable to hold back the anger bubbling up inside me. "I'll kill them."

Kristen jolts at the sound of my voice, curling herself away from me and toward Rae. Rae shoots me a warning look, bares her teeth at me, and then pointedly jerks her eyes toward home.

Like hell I'm leaving her alone.

Rather than obeying her, I rise to my feet, flicking off my flashlight, and take a few steps back. This seems to satisfy both women because Rae stops glowering at me and Kristen's shuddering lessens.

I want to help, but Rae's made it clear she's got this.

All I can do is watch with horrified interest as Rae inspects Kristen's wounds while murmuring soft things to her that I'm not privy to hear.

"Ryder is going to pick you up, Kristen, okay? He's my brother and he's safe. He would never hurt you," Rae assures her. "We have to get you back home so we can take a look at your wounds."

The woman doesn't put up any argument, so I shake away my daze and slowly step forward. Rae peels out of her flannel shirt, leaving her in a too-tight T-shirt that puts my teeth on edge, and wraps it around Kristen's waist, covering her up. As gently as I can, I slide my arms beneath the battered woman.

Kristen whimpers and then starts to cry as I scoop her up off the ground. She doesn't weigh much more than Rae does and is similar in build. My chest aches thinking about if it were my sister in her place instead. Disgust ripples through me and I have to swallow a furious growl.

Whoever did this must pay.

We *will* make them pay.

Hours later, Kristen is soundly sleeping in the big house under Mom's watch, safely out of harm's way. Dad and Michael chased everyone out of there once we brought her in, the two of them assessing her wounds. Now that she's stable, clean, and medicated, they both return to the bonfire outside where everyone sits quietly, a ripple of fear quaking through the entire group.

"Who could do this?" I demand, addressing my father with a mixture of disgust and disbelief.

Dad's lips thin out and he shakes his head. "I think Michael can answer that."

Michael scrubs a palm over his face and sighs heavily. "It has to be…*them*."

"Them?" Ronan asks from beside Logan, who's damn near catatonic.

Owen and Michael share a heavy look before Michael speaks up again. "We had some people following us. A couple of men. A little too friendly and gave us weird vibes. Owen and I ran them off, but I don't think we could quite shake them."

My blood runs cold knowing they led actual monsters back to our home.

"You didn't think to share this important tidbit of information?" I growl. "Seriously? It could have been one of my sisters!"

"Enough," Dad barks. "It wasn't. But it *was* Logan's wife. It doesn't matter the who, just that it happened."

I cut my eyes over to Logan. He's somber and frowning, but that's not what has my hackles raised. Ronan is standing all too close to him, whispering to him as though he's comforting him in some secret way no one else is allowed to hear. For some reason, it pisses me off. I should feel bad for the guy since his wife was kidnapped, beaten to hell, and raped, most likely by two different men.

And yet…

All I notice is how Ronan slips a comforting arm around Logan's waist, hugging him to his side. It rankles to see Logan nearly collapse into my brother's hug.

I don't like the way they touch.

These people are bad news.

Logan may be a decent guy, but his people brought this into our backyard. They led some vicious men to our home where it could have been Rae or Destiny out there rather than one of their own. Twice now, my family's safety has been in jeopardy because of these people.

I'll be damned if I let it happen a third time.

Michael says something to Logan that has him peeling himself—reluctantly—out of Ronan's arms. Choosing my brother over whatever the men are going to discuss, I make a beeline over to him. He frowns at me when I grab his bicep and tug him away from the brightness of the fire and into the shadows of our yard.

"This is so fucked-up," I murmur before pulling Ronan against my chest and hugging him. "So fucked-up."

Ronan is stiff at first but quickly melts into my embrace. His arms snake around me, squeezing me tight. My heart thunders wildly in my chest.

When I'd grabbed him, all I'd cared about was getting him away from Logan, but now that I have him in my arms, a different sensation tingles through me.

Relief. Happiness. Warmth.

The adrenaline that'd been running through me all day floods out of me and I sag against him. My nose finds his neck and I inhale the smoky campfire scent that hides his usual cinnamon smell. The urge to lick his skin there to see if he tastes the same as he smells is brief and frankly confusing. Somehow I manage to keep my tongue in my mouth.

"It could have been Rae," I whisper. "It kills me to think of her like how we found Kristen."

Ronan tenses and his arms hug me impossibly tighter. "It wasn't and for that we can be thankful."

It seems like maybe we've gone long past an appropriate hug time, but I can't find it in me to pull away. Ronan doesn't try either. Luckily, it's late and dark, allowing us a rare moment of privacy.

In this moment, I can almost pretend everything is fine. That there aren't monsters or trespassers threatening my family. That tonight is any other ordinary night in the Jamison household. That my biggest life problem is Raegan stealing my knife.

I hold onto the moment just a little while longer because the second I let Ronan go, the harsh reality will intrude once more.

We won't be safe again until these people are gone.

And, starting tomorrow, I'm going to do whatever it takes to make that happen.

CHAPTER FOURTEEN

raegan

I'S DAYS LIKE THESE THAT REALLY MAKE ME WISH we lived in town near Wild and his family. Not that I would willingly choose to be near that douchebag, but it would mean access to hospitals and the police.

As it stands, we have a woman who may or may not be going into labor, a teenage boy badly injured after a bear mauling yesterday, and a traumatized woman who was snatched from her bed last night and God only knows what happened to her.

We are so not equipped to handle this.

My parents are trying, though. For people who don't like outsiders, they've really stepped up to help them. Like letting them move their camp last night within our fenced-in boundaries and set up their tents on the west lawn near Dad's workshop. I slept a lot easier last night knowing CJ and the rest weren't going to get hurt. Everyone is as safe as they can be thanks to Dad's generosity.

At least, within the week, Uncle Atticus will be here for a visit, bringing much-needed medicines and supplies that we can use.

CJ tosses a twig my way and flashes me a grin. I smile back, shaking my head. Despite all the trauma everyone has been through in the past few days, I can count on CJ to make things feel somewhat normal. Ryder hates him and would probably beat his ass if he had an opportunity alone with him, but I like CJ. Not to mention, he's a good kisser.

While the men are hashing out a plan to hunt down whomever hurt Kristen, the memory of my kiss with CJ distracts me. It started out sweet—just a peck on the lips—and when I laughed at the surprise of it, he plunged his tongue into my mouth. At first it felt weird, but the way he groaned with such fiery need and pressed his body against mine, I got dizzy with pleasure.

I felt CJ's hard penis pressing against me, which made me a little nervous and a lot happy, but then Ryder, like always, ruined all my fun.

I still don't understand why Ryder hates CJ so much. Even Destiny has thawed when it comes to the new people and is now sitting near Jace, nodding at whatever he whispers to her. These people are nice and funny and most importantly a break from the monotony.

As if cued into my thoughts, CJ meets my gaze, pointedly looks toward Ronan's cabin, and winks. His suggestion is loud and clear: Let's slip away so we can make out. A warm flush tickles over my skin at the thought of his tongue in my mouth again.

But then I feel it.

Ryder's glare.

He watches me with fire in his eyes, jaw clenching furiously. Yesterday, he was so pissed. CJ's lucky he didn't earn himself a black eye. Had Ronan not intervened, I'm sure Ryder would have decked him.

But why?

Because he doesn't want me to be happy?

Or is it something else?

My thoughts flit back to when Ryder had me pinned as he attempted to steal my knife. He'd been hard just like CJ. Maybe he hates CJ because he secretly wishes it were him kissing me instead.

The thought is alarming, confusing, and annoying.

CJ attempts to get my attention again, making an exaggerated gesture toward the cabin. Tempting, but not with Ryder watching my every move. I purse my lips and give CJ a quick shake of my head, turning him down. For now. He frowns, giving me the saddest puppy dog eyes I've ever seen. Not one to be guilted into doing anything, I dart my stare back over to Ryder.

He's no longer seemingly pissed. Ryder has relaxed, sprawling out his long, muscular jean-clad legs out in front of him and now wears a satisfied smirk. His bright blue eyes twinkle in the afternoon sun. Normally, I don't look at him with more than typical sibling annoyance, but today I notice what someone like Mya sees in him.

My brother is beautiful.

Tall and strong.

His dark hair is messy—always—but it's as though he planned it that way. It suits him. My fingers twitch at the thought of running them through the mahogany strands in an attempt to tame them. The stubble along his jaw indicates just how much of a man he's becoming. It seems like just last year he was boyish and antagonistic and immature. As of late, he's far from boyish if his big, hard cock has any say so. While he's still one to push my buttons, it's not unwelcome. I kind of look forward to our bickering because he challenges me in a way no one else can or will.

"…rotating perimeter watch shifts until we catch those bastards," Dad says, cutting through my blatant admiration of my brother. "Any questions?"

I blink away the haze I'd skipped off into and look over at my father. He stands between Michael and Owen, arms crossed over his muscular chest, waiting for anyone to speak up.

"I'm going to hunt them down," Ryder vows. "We leave at dusk?"

"I'll be ready," I tell them both. "I'm a good tracker."

Dad scowls at me. "Were you even listening, sunshine? No women are leaving this area until we catch them. I'll be damned if I let something happen to you."

I gape at him in shock. "I'm not a woman. I'm just me. I can help. Dad, you have to let me help!"

"No," Dad growls with such vehemence the hairs

on my arms stand on end. "You'll look after your siblings where it's safe."

"Seriously?" I hiss in disbelief. "You're not letting me go because I'm a girl? That's sexist!"

CJ snorts a laugh but then flinches when I glower at him. Mya shoots me a taunting smirk that makes me want to smack it off her face.

"Keep it up," Dad warns, "and I'll finish this with my belt."

Mya smothers a giggle, covering her mouth with her hand. My blood boils at the injustice of it all. Not only is Dad humiliating me in front of everyone, but he's being incredibly unfair. I know I promised Ronan once upon a time I'd never leave him or our family, but it's times like these that I'm reminded of why I want to run far, far away from here.

"How are Carter and Kristen doing?" Ronan asks, my savior for wanting to take the attention off me. I could hug him if I weren't so infuriated. "Are they going to live?"

Michael interjects this time. "Carter is in a lot of pain. We've cleaned his wounds and stitched him up, but it'll be a while yet before he's out of the woods. It's important we watch for infection, which could be the real problem."

"And Kristen?" Ronan urges. "We're all so worried about her."

A spike of irritation burns up my spine as Ronan

pats Logan's back. Something about the way he comforts the man has my teeth on edge.

"Kristen," Dad says with a harsh sigh, "will live. Hers is less physical and more psychological. What she went through…" His features harden. "Let's just say she's going to need everyone's love and support to get her through this."

Logan buries his face in his palms, devastation consuming him. I can't imagine the horror of what Kristen went through. She must have been so terrified. Anger ignites in my belly and I'm furious all over again. I should be out there helping with the hunting efforts to bring those psychos down.

"Now that that's settled," Dad barks out, "the men going on the hunt can meet me by the gate in just a few. Everyone else can work on supper and getting the children settled for the evening. We'll dine together and then we'll be on our way."

I watch with disgust as everyone who went on the search for Kristen last night stands and then makes their way over to the gate. Everyone except me. It's so unfair. I'm once again reduced to a cook and babysitter.

Yep, I am so leaving this hell hole the first chance I get.

Dinner was a somber affair. Well, aside from my loud younger siblings making their usual ruckus of course.

I was forced to wash dishes alongside Mya, which was torture in and of itself. When I finally managed to slip away, it wasn't to find CJ to give him a farewell kiss.

It was to be alone with my simmering thoughts.

Darkness has blanketed our homestead and the only light illuminating the area is from the big house and the bonfire where people were once again gathered around after filling their bellies. I make a beeline away from the light and let the shadows swallow me up.

At least in the darkness, no one can see how my chin quivers and tears prickle my eyes. I want to scream and throw a fit until Dad gives in, but deep down I know he won't. He'll whip me in front of everyone to make a point if he has to. Not interested in that whatsoever.

I lean against the wall of Ronan's cabin between his and Ryder's. It's impossible to see here and I'm one hundred percent fine with that. I allow myself to feel sorry for myself, sniffling softly. A sob catches in my throat, but I swallow it down until it becomes a tiny, nearly silent mewl.

Crack.

The sound of a twig breaking has me stiffening. It could be CJ come to find me, eager for a kiss. But CJ doesn't have that uncanny ability to make my blood boil like Ryder does. I can sense his presence without even seeing him.

He prowls toward me, too quiet for his own good, until I feel the warmth of his body inches from mine.

I don't speak and hope he didn't hear me nearly break down in a fit of tears.

His hand finds my face, curling around my jaw. I want to snarl something cruel to him and wrench away from his firm hold. Instead, I lift my chin, staring into the darkness of where I think his face might be.

Why is he even here?

Why is he even touching me?

I wait for him to get on with it. To taunt me and terrorize me. To shove it into my face that he gets to go because he has a stupid fucking penis and I have to stay here with my useless good-for-nothing-except-making-babies vagina.

He doesn't.

His nose touches mine. A small brush of skin against skin that has me pausing. All angry thoughts dissipate as an unwanted thrill tickles through me.

He runs his thumb along my cheek. When he feels the proof of a tear gone rogue, he rests his forehead to mine. The move is such a comforting one, I close my eyes. Ronan is my comfort, my savior, my best friend. Ryder is just Ryder. A brat. My nemesis.

But I know that's not completely true.

Ryder is my equal whether Dad wants to believe it or not. Ryder understands my desire to be free in the wilderness, enjoying the hunt and the freedom to run wild. We get each other on a level me and Ronan don't.

Is this why Ryder is here? Because he knows it's unfair and that I'm crushed by being left behind?

"I wanted to go," I croak out, hating how shaking my voice is. "I wanted to help."

He rubs his thumb back and forth over my wet cheek as though he can't stop himself from the soothing action. It dizzies me and distracts me as well.

"I know," he rasps out, warm breath tickling over my face. "I'm sorry."

His genuine, pained response has me relaxing. Maybe Ryder isn't always out to get me or be better than me. Maybe he actually wants me to be by his side.

I grab onto his shirt, not entirely sure what I plan to do. I could push him away from me. If he'd uttered anything cruel, it'd have been so easy to do just that. But since he's being comforting, I find myself tugging instead.

Would he be hard again if he pressed into me?

The thought is exhilarating and makes my heart stumble. I tug harder, the curiosity overwhelming me. He grunts, losing his footing in the dark, and crashes rather painfully into me. His mouth, open and panting heavily, is pressed against my cheek.

Neither of us speaks a word. He sucks in a sharp breath the second his penis goes hard between us. Triumph surges through me and I have no idea why. I like that I can make this happen to him. It makes me struggle to find my own breath to fill my lungs.

He shifts, his hips slightly moving, making his penis dig into me. It's so wonderfully hard. Like a thick stick made of river rock. I have the urge to put my hand around him and rub on it.

Now we're both struggling to breathe.

"Y-Your cock is hard," I whisper, unable to keep silent any longer.

He groans, nuzzling his nose against mine. "My cock is out of control."

"Need me to help you get it under control?" I ask, a tremor of anticipation running through me, though I have no idea what that would entail.

He groans and his lips peck at my cheek. Heat floods through me at the simple kiss. There was no tongue involved and yet I find myself replaying it over and over and over again inside my mind.

"I have to go, Rae. I just needed to make sure you were okay first."

My heart squeezes in my chest. It's probably the nicest thing Ryder has ever said to me. Everything about him feels nice right now. His body, his words, his mouth, *his cock*.

I want to kiss him on the mouth with tongue and teeth.

When I start to slide my hand down his stomach to feel his hard cock and help him get it settled, he lets out a strangled sound and then stumbles away from me. The loss is immediate, chilly air penetrating my flesh and soaking into my bones. I cross my arms over my chest, hoping to hold onto some of his leftover warmth.

"Ryder," I whine, frustration in my voice.

I want him to stay. I want to keep exploring what ever this strange thing is between us.

"We, uh, can't," Ryder mutters. "That can't happen."

He takes off, stomping away from me without another word. I'm bewildered by the fact he knew exactly what I was thinking. Did I say it out loud?

Shame bleeds through the lingering pleasure of our stolen moment, reminding me that he's right.

Whatever that was can't happen.

He's my brother.

A sister and brother aren't meant to be anything more than friends.

Now, if only I could convince my pattering heart and trembling body…

CHAPTER FIFTEEN

ronan

THE CLOUDS ABOVE ARE MENACING AND WARN of an impending storm. Because of the cloud cover, it's nearly impossible to see in the dark forest. Dad and Owen lead the way with Rowdy and Ryder trailing behind. Me and Logan bring up the rear. The other hunting group went out farther south so we could cover more ground in the overall direction we think the rapists went.

Since we don't want to give ourselves away, Dad has instructed we hunt without flashlights or lanterns. All that can be heard is the crunching of boots on sticks and fallen limbs and leaves. Occasionally, I hear a grunt or a whisper.

We travel this way for several hours. If I had to guess, it's nearing midnight. The wind has picked up and I'm glad I layered up on clothes. My backpack grows heavier with each step, making me wish we could take a break soon.

"We can catch up," Logan murmurs, voice soft and barely audible. "Let's sit for a minute."

The sounds of the others grow more and more distant as we come to a halt. Soon, it's quiet again aside from our panting and the crickets singing nearby. Logan captures my bicep in his firm hold, sending a hot thrill shooting down my spine straight to my dick.

Not now, man.

Of all the times to lust after someone, this is absolutely the worst time as we hunt down his wife's assailants. I attempt to squash all sexual thoughts as Logan guides me to a fallen log. We sit down on it, close enough our thighs brush against each other's. Logan rummages around in his pack before he pulls something out. In the darkness, I can't exactly see what it is, but when I smell something savory, I imagine it's beef jerky.

A strip of beef brushes against my lips. Is he feeding me or did he mean to hand it to me but some made it to my mouth instead?

I reach up and take hold of the offering, my fingers accidentally brushing over his. He lets out a soft breath and I wonder if he's onto me. I'm obviously stupidly pining over this man and am having trouble hiding it.

Distracting myself, I take a bite of the beef jerky and attempt to think of anything except the nearness of Logan or the touch of his thigh against mine. Anything.

"How does your dad feel about you being gay?" Logan asks, voice a mere whisper.

I nearly choke on the beef jerky. I manage to swallow it down and then steel my spine. "W-What?"

Logan chuckles and the sound reverberates through every bone in my body. "Bisexual perhaps? Hell, maybe you don't even know for sure. I remember being your age and not knowing what the fuck to do about my traitorous dick."

I don't know what to say to his confession, nor do I know how to react. Am I that obvious to everyone around me?

"I don't know what you mean," I lie, shifting uncomfortably.

His palm covers my thigh just above my knee and he squeezes. "I'm not an idiot, Ronan. I know how you feel about me."

Is he angry?

Is this what this is? Him confronting me?

"I'm sorry," I choke out, fear seizing my throat. "Don't tell my dad."

"Sorry?" His breath tickles the side of my face as he leans in. "Why are you sorry?"

I don't know why I'm sorry, just that I am.

Mostly, though, I don't want anyone to know.

"Can we talk about something else?" I plead, voice cracking.

Logan goes silent for a moment and then he sighs. "Like how I'm bisexual and I think you're hot as fuck, which confuses the hell out of me since I'm supposed to be a happily married man? I'm hunting down my wife's rapists, for fuck's sake, and all I can think about is you."

His words both thrill and horrify me.

It's one thing when it's all in my head. It's a whole other when it's spoken aloud.

"You think I'm hot?" I can't help but grin in the darkness. It helps not being able to see his face.

He chuckles. "Don't play coy. Of course I do. You have no fucking idea how much I want you."

I turn toward him, now wishing I could see his eyes—to see proof of his want for me in them. All I see is more darkness. But then I feel it. Soft lips brushing over mine.

"Logan," I breathe, unable to stop myself from leaning into him.

His strong hand finds the back of my head, drawing me to him as his tongue enters my mouth. I groan in shock and then pleasure as he slicks it over my own tongue. It's the most delicious and wonderful thing I've ever tasted. I don't even care much for beef jerky, but the taste of it on Logan's tongue is addictive and leaves me desperate for more.

He kisses me with a need that's feral and possessive. All I can do is willingly become his captive to this all-consuming kiss. I moan against his mouth and nip at his bottom lip. His palm has crept farther up my thigh and one of his fingertips is touching my dick through the denim.

I've died and gone to heaven.

Something cracks nearby in the forest, causing Logan to pull back from my mouth. We're both panting heavily, out of breath from our spectacular kiss. I revel in the memory of it, ignoring reality for just a few moments longer.

"Fuck," Logan curses. "I'm sorry. Fuck, I'm so sorry. You just tempt me so goddamn much."

"It's okay," I murmur. "I liked it."

"I did too, but…"

He has a wife.

He. Has. A. Wife.

I'm a monster. Who kisses a man when he's in such a vulnerable position? Me apparently.

"But we shouldn't have," I finish for him, voice dripping in self-loathing.

"No," Logan agrees. "We shouldn't have. I mean, me and Kristen have our problems. We're not perfect, but I committed myself to her."

Shame floods through me, making me want to drown in it.

"I understand," I choke out. I do. I understand, but I also hate it.

"If things were different," Logan says, gently caressing my thigh, "we could. We could and we'd be so fucking good at it."

Filthy images of us naked and fucking fill my mind. It doesn't help that his finger keeps teasing my dick through my jeans.

Why is my life this way?

"You're perfect, Ronan," Logan croons. "So fucking perfect and one day you're going to make a man very happy."

A man.

He acknowledges that it'll be a man. Just not him.

"My parents would never allow it," I whisper. "They will be disgusted with me."

His breath tickles over my face, so close I think he might kiss me again. He doesn't. "Sometimes we do things that make us happy even if we have to keep them a secret."

"Like the kiss we shared?"

"Yeah, Ronan, like that. It's our secret."

His hand drifts closer, not farther away, stroking me over my throbbing length. My mind goes completely blank aside from the way he incinerates me with his touch.

I want more from him.

I need more.

I need it all.

"Logan—"

"Shh," he hisses, voice sharp as he freezes. "Fucking hell! It's them!"

He jolts away from me, cursing as he fumbles

with the zipper of his pack. Then I hear the telltale sign of a bullet being chambered in a handgun.

Pop! Pop! Pop!

The sudden assault of sound and the three quick flashes of light have me crying out in shock. Logan tears off into the woods, crashing through anything and everything in his way. I draw my own .45 and hurry after him, a little more careful in my steps than him.

Logan is relentless as he chases after the men who hurt his wife. Guilt consumes me, but I squash it down in favor of helping him find those monsters. We're searching for a good twenty minutes before a string of familiar voices are calling to us.

"Ronan! Logan!"

"Over here," I call out to Dad. "Logan saw them and managed to shoot at them. I don't think they're injured."

A flashlight flickers on and Dad's face is illuminated nearby. He casts the glow my way, temporarily blinding me. I squint against the harsh brightness.

"Did you see them?" Dad asks. "Which way did they go?"

Logan walks over to us, vibrating with anger. When he glances at me, some of the fury melts away and his eyes flash with an unspoken apology.

Right.

We'd been kissing and he was in the middle of touching my dick before we were interrupted. As soon as Dad starts drilling Logan with questions, I step away from the group, sucking in a calming breath of air.

I jolt in surprise when someone touches my shoulder. When I realize it's Ryder, I relax a bit, but not entirely. He turns on his own flashlight, pointing it at the ground between us. There's just enough glow for me to make out his features.

Concern is the main expression twisting his features. But once he quickly assesses me and determines I'm safe, his eyes narrow.

I squirm under his scrutiny, hoping like hell he won't know what I've done. Forcing myself to hold his gaze, I pretend everything is fine aside from my flaming hot cheeks and lips that feel slightly raw from the bristles of Logan's beard on my skin.

It's so obvious.

Dammit!

It's clear when Ryder comes to a conclusion of what must be close to the truth because his intense gaze burns hot with anger.

Does he hate me now for what I've done?

Ryder steps closer, his nostrils flaring. He sniffs—actually fucking sniffs—my face like he can smell Logan's scent on me. He must pick up on whatever clue he's hunting for because a low rumble echoes from his throat.

"Are you fucking kidding me right now?" he hisses, anger flashing dark in his eyes.

I swivel around, quickly making sure no one is around who can hear. The men are all speaking in hushed voices with Logan at the center. It's just me and Ryder.

The embarrassment threatens to swallow me whole. I don't know what to say or how to explain what just happened. All I know is I liked it—no, loved it—but also know it's really wrong.

"Did you suck his dick?" Ryder demands in a barely audible whisper, practically snarling the question.

I swallow hard and shake my head vehemently. "N-No. Ryder, calm down."

"Calm down?" His eyes widen in disbelief. "Some fucker is seducing my brother and I'm supposed to calm the fuck down?"

His voice has risen, but thankfully still not loud enough for the group to hear above their own talking. I grab hold of his hand, pleading with my eyes.

"It was just a kiss," I blurt out. Pain slices through my chest as Ryder flinches like he's been struck. "It was nothing."

Lies.

It was everything.

Everything I'll never have, but I so desperately want.

He shakes his head, betrayal making his face

crumble into a devastated frown. I don't understand why he's so upset with me over a stupid kiss!

Not a stupid kiss.

A perfect, wonderful, soul-destroying kiss.

"Ryder—"

He swings a hand my way and for a second I think he might hit me. Of course he doesn't. Instead, he shoves his middle finger in my face. I blink at it, stung by the action.

"Whatever," he snaps. "Have fun ruining your life all by yourself."

With those words, he storms away back to the group. Pain slams into my chest a million times worse than if he'd actually hit me.

What have I done?

CHAPTER SIXTEEN

ryder

"*IT WAS JUST A KISS. IT WAS NOTHING.*"

His words repeat over and over and over again in my head, making me angrier by the second. It wasn't just a kiss. It was an invasion. A hostile takeover. An act of war.

Logan is preying on my brother and he's falling for it.

I want to know what Logan's plans are for Ronan. Does he think he can fuck him on the side while his wife recovers from being gang raped? Everything in me screams at me to tell Dad what happened. But as much as that entices me so I can watch Dad go apeshit on Logan, I bite my tongue.

He'll go apeshit on Ronan too.

Wind whistles through the trees and I have to plant my feet firmly into the ground to keep from swaying. Rain is imminent. I can smell the earthy ozone scent in the air as pine needles and leaves dance across my face from the wind.

"Rowdy, take the boys to that clearing we passed," Dad instructs. "Me, Owen, and Logan can set some traps nearby. They're close and with this storm rolling in, they won't get far. It'll be easier to be stealthy with just a few of us."

Rowdy nods and then turns on his flashlight, motioning for us to follow him. I'm not sure where CJ and Jace are as we haven't run into the other group yet. Honestly, I hope they stay far away from me or I'll use CJ's face as a means to beat out my frustrations.

And frustrations I have aplenty.

I've been obsessing over the fact that me and Rae had a moment earlier. A sick, twisted, wrong moment.

Fuck, it had been thrilling, though.

I could have kissed her. I wanted to. I'm almost positive she would have let me. And the way her hand crept down toward my cock.

Fuck. Fuck. Fuck.

I wanted that moment with her so damn badly.

My dick has been half hard since. That is, until I learned Logan's been making out with my damn brother. Nothing like betrayal to kill a boner.

What's my fixation on my siblings lately?

Am I confusing our deepening friendships with something sinister like lust?

Could I really jeopardize my life by making a move

on my sister or staking some caveman claim on my brother?

Yes.

The truth is a punch to the gut and dangerous. My mind is a wild, chaotic mess. I need to keep myself away from these situations if I have any hope of navigating them. I can't be pissed off if my brother kisses another man. I should be happy for him.

Nah.

Fuck that.

I still want to kill Logan.

If CJ were here, I'd want to kill him too.

Fuck my life.

"Everything good?" Rowdy asks, voice low. "You mad we didn't catch them yet?"

"Hell yeah," I growl. Among other more infuriating things…

"Me too. We'll get them eventually. These woods may be vast, but we know them like the back of our hands. Those fuckers won't have a chance."

I wish I could fixate on catching the bad guys, but my mind keeps circling back to the moment with Raegan and disgusting thoughts of Logan mauling my brother. With my mind elsewhere, we come up on the clearing in no time. Rowdy tosses me the tent bag after unstrapping it from his backpack.

"Set this up. I'll take first watch while you guys sleep. No campfire. We don't need those assholes to know where we're at." He hands Ronan a battery-operated lantern. "Use this sparingly while he puts the tent up and then lights off."

At least having a task allows me to focus on something else that doesn't make me blind with rage. Despite the increasingly vicious wind, I manage to erect the tent by myself while Ronan wisely stands aside, holding the lantern closer to me whenever I need the light to see.

It starts to rain softly at first, but then the clouds release buckets of it all at once. Ronan snaps the lantern shut, immersing us in total darkness. I manage to fumble my way into the tent and he quickly follows behind.

The silence between us is oppressive.

A nasty, evil beast standing between us, snarling at us both.

I hate it.

I hate him.

"Ry," Ronan croaks out. "Can we talk?"

Scoffing, I drop my backpack to the floor and set to rummaging for my sleeping bag. "There's nothing to say."

He's quiet as we situate our bedding. We're both soaked and getting everything wet from our clothes, but if anything, it cools off some of my anger.

I sprawl out on one side of the tent, trying like hell to ignore my brother. He swallows audibly and the fabric of his sleeping bag makes a swishing sound as he attempts to get comfortable.

I bet he wishes Logan were here so they could suck each other's dicks and fuck.

My hands curl into tight fists. I want to punch something. Someone. Ronan would be the obvious choice since he's within reach, but I refrain.

The tent shudders against the wind and the rain pelting it grows louder. I wonder if Dad will cut his expedition short and come crawl into the sanctity of our tent soon. At least then we'd have a physical barrier to keep me from knocking some sense into Ronan.

"I know you're mad…" He sighs heavily. "I just don't understand why."

I open my mouth to tell him exactly why. Then I clamp it shut. Honestly, I don't know why I'm so angry. Logan is a dick and Ronan deserves better. End of story.

Is that the truth, though?

Guilt swarms in my gut like a hive of angry bees. It's not the full truth.

The truth is, I'm jealous.

Ronan is my brother.

Mine.

If he was going to experiment with a man, it should've been me. Someone he could trust to keep his secret. Someone who could protect him.

Logan is a liability.

A fucking snake.

He seems the type to gather information on people to use it against them later. Something about that man just rubs me up the wrong way. It's a sixth sense. A gut feeling.

Ronan reaches across the tent and his fingers brush

over my fisted hand. I freeze at his touch. His fingers are ice-cold. My first thought is to gather his hand in both of mine to warm it up.

Instead, I remain still, fist clenched tight.

"Talk to me," Ronan pleads, voice hoarse with emotion. "Don't do this to me. It fucking hurts."

His words lash at me, making me wince. Hurt? How the fuck does he think I feel? I'm destroyed. With Rae, knowing she kissed CJ, I was mad and protective. But it was different. Raegan is smart and has good intuition. She kissed him because it was something to do—an act of rebellion. Not because she actually likes him and wants to have all his babies. CJ, though annoying as shit, isn't a real threat.

Ronan is completely different.

I can feel him getting sucked into a current that'll take him to places I can't swim from. Dark, deep places that'll drown him. He'll come back broken and different, just like Rowdy did when he spent time in town.

Logan will break my brother.

He's the bigger threat. Ronan falling for it so easily fucking hurts. It's like he's willingly allowing Logan to pull him away from me just because he wants to experiment with a man.

I wasn't lying the other night in my cabin when I told him it should be me.

Sure, we were laughing and joking, but I meant it.

"He makes me feel desired," Ronan whispers.

"Something I never thought that could happen to me because…"

He likes men.

Unable to keep quiet, I roll toward him, unfurling my fist. His fingers desperately thread between mine, seeking the comfort he needs. Because I love him, I let him take in this moment.

"He's going to hurt you," I murmur. "He's going to hurt you and you're going to let him."

Ronan sighs heavily. "I know. There's no good way it could turn out. He has a wife. I'm just a temporary indulgence."

Ronan deserves to be someone's forever sustenance.

Not a bite to be swallowed down when a craving should arise.

"Don't kiss him," I say, tugging on his hand. "Please don't kiss him."

Ronan scoots closer, bringing his body heat with him. I pull his hand to my chest, squeezing it tight. He snuggles up to my side and it feels right. It's where he belongs. I fucking know this. Something inside my chest releases and a soul-soaking calm washes over me.

"Promise me you'll never kiss him again." My voice cracks, splintered with pain and misery. "I can't fucking stand the thought of it."

I expect him to demand to know why it bothers me so much.

I could admit it to him. That it should be me instead.

"I promise," Ronan whispers. "It felt right in the moment, but now all I feel is guilt."

Bringing our conjoined hands to my mouth, I kiss his cold knuckles one by one.

"His, uh, fingers…" He trails off, shuddering. "And then his hand…"

Possessiveness poisons my every cell, pouring through my veins like molten lava. Before I can consider my actions, I roll onto my side, bringing my hand down to his dick.

"He touched you here?"

Ronan groans, his dick quickly thickening. "Ryder…"

"You want to be touched, you come to me," I growl, squeezing his length through his soaked jeans. "You let me give you what you need. That's what brothers are for. We take care of each other."

A small moan escapes him and his hips thrust toward my hand. I rub him roughly through his clothes, doing it just the way I like it. He's not complaining. His breaths come out sharp and quick. My own cock hardens and several filthy thoughts flitter through my mind. I ignore them all, focusing on just him.

"Ryder, Ryder, Ryder," he chants, over and over again in the barest whisper. "Oh God."

"*I* make you feel good. Not him."

"Y-Yes. Fuck."

Pleasure floods through me at his agreement. I work him easily into a frenzy that has him squeezing my other hand so tight I'm surprised my fingers don't snap off. And then, with a sigh of ultimate relief, he tenses.

His dick pulsates in my grip. Knowing he's soaking the inside of his boxers with cum has me grinning stupidly. Everything's too raw with our emotions right now, but I ache to tease him about it. Later, when he takes a piss and sees the sticky evidence of what we did, he'll think of me. Not Logan. Me.

"Anything you need, Ro, you come to me," I remind him. "No one but us needs to know. It's safe for you this way."

"Thank you."

His breathy words are so sweet I can't help but seek his face out in the dark. I press a kiss to his damp skin, my face bumping his glasses in the process. Gently, I reach up and pluck them off his face before setting them on his chest.

He turns slightly toward me and this time my lips brush over his. They're slick and he smells like rain. His lips pucker and I mimic him, pressing against them with a chaste kiss.

Logan probably kissed him with tongue.

I'm about to suggest it when Ronan thanks me again and then rolls over to his side, his back to me. I wrap an arm around his waist, burying my face in his wet curls that smell uniquely him.

I'll show him how much better I can be.

He'll never have to think about that prick ever again.

I'll do whatever it takes to keep Ronan away from Logan. Even if it means fucking my big brother to keep him happy. I may not know exactly what that entails between two men, but I'd do it for him.

Anything for Ronan.

CHAPTER SEVENTEEN

raegan

THIS IS TORTURE.

And, quite frankly, a glimpse of my future if my parents have anything to say about it.

They want me home, taking care of kids, cooking and cleaning, while the men go out into the wilderness to do the real jobs.

I hate Wild Knox, but the more I consider it, the more he feels like a viable option to escape this world I've been born into.

Leaving means leaving Ronan and Ryder, though, and that doesn't sit well with me.

"You're not typically my brother's type," Mya snarks as she stirs sauce on the stove. "He usually goes for someone much sweeter."

"Apparently, he likes me just as I am." I flash her a saccharine smile. "Sour."

She rolls her eyes, turning her back to me. Mom is too distracted with all these women and children around to pay attention to this girl, who seems to enjoy tormenting me.

"You're just a phase," she huffs. "It's not like he's going to ask you to marry him after playing tonsil hockey."

I don't know what tonsil hockey is, but I wasn't born yesterday.

"Maybe I should let him suck on my boobs since he's so fond of my tongue," I spit out. "Trust me, he'll want to marry me then."

I'm totally just making stuff up, but it sounds badass and it pisses her off, which was the point. She tosses the spoon onto the counter before spinning around to glower at me. The girl is shorter than me. Scrawny too. I could take her in a fight.

"If he marries you, it'll be for one thing. Procreation. Certainly not recreation. Virgins are so overrated." She eyes me up and down critically. "Have you even heard of makeup? Try it sometime, wild girl."

Her insult hits, but I don't let it show, shrugging instead. "At least I don't have to hide what a hideous beast I am unlike some people."

Of course Mom walks into the kitchen at that exact moment.

Of course she does.

I sigh, ready for her words to lash at me, but she shoots a warning look to both of us before gesturing toward the food. "Rae, sunshine, can you take Stacey some food. I doubt the others will eat, but I know she's probably hungry. Might do the others good to have someone different besides me to visit."

Sunshine?

Usually that title is what Dad calls me. I can't help but feel like my mom just secretly sided with me, which means maybe she heard Mya being nasty to me first. I helplessly fight a grin as I make up a plate of spaghetti for Stacey. When my family works together as a team, I'm a lot more hesitant to up and leave them. Even Mom, who's my least favorite person here besides Kota.

"Boo!"

Kota, the little demon in question, launches himself from behind the sofa the second I pass with the tray of food. I nearly dump it all over his filthy head. He'd deserve it too!

"Move, you little shit!"

He sticks his tongue out at me. "Or what?"

"Since Dad's belt doesn't scare you, maybe I'll drag you outside the gate and let the bears eat you like they did Carter." I hiss at him to drive home that threat.

His face contorts into an uneasy frown before he scurries off, no doubt off to tattle on me. Whatever. I don't care.

Declan peeks around the corner of the sofa, staring up at me with horror in his eyes. *Sorry, little man, but your big brother had that coming to him.* I bare my teeth playfully at him. He screeches and then starts to cry. Whoops. Mom's problem now.

When I make it to Destiny's and my room, I peek

in the door that's slightly ajar. Carter lies on a cot at the foot of Destiny's bed where Stacey is sitting up, propped against pillows, reading Dawson a picture book. I dart my stare over to my bed. Kristen, covered to her chin in a blanket, stares up at the ceiling, not moving. Slowly, I enter the room and drift toward Kristen, watching her eyes to see if she'll blink.

Maybe she's dead.

"That smells divine, sweetie," Stacey says, making me jump in surprise. "Oh, sorry. Didn't mean to startle you."

"Bababa," Dawson says in baby talk no one but him and Dad can understand.

Stacey chuckles. "Apologies, Mr. Dawson. We'll continue reading."

I stare at them and frown. Mom probably enjoys having this bedridden pregnant lady to help her babysit the kids. Dawson seems taken with Stacey. Maybe she can take him with her whenever she leaves and give the rest of us a break.

"Here's some food for you," I state, setting the tray down on the table beside her bed. "I was going to bring some for the other two, but Mom said they wouldn't be hungry."

Stacey hands the book to Dawson and gives me a sad smile. "Carter is in a lot of pain. Thankfully, Devon had some painkillers to give to him. He's sleeping a lot, which is good for healing."

I glance over at the boy, who seems much smaller

than he did a couple of days ago. He's so fragile and broken. I wonder if he'll ever heal up.

"I hope he feels better soon," I say, forcing a smile. "What about her?"

Stacey grimaces. "I don't know. I'm sure that was awful what she went through. I can't even imagine." She chews on her bottom lip and her eyes well with tears. "Poor Logan. I know he's just beating himself up over this."

"What does Logan have to do with it?" I demand, crossing my arms over my chest. "She should be able to protect herself."

She shakes her head. "As her husband, Logan has a duty. I've seen the way your father treats your mother. With our clan, it's the same. The men protect the women and children. We provide them with comfort, love, and support."

My lip curls up in disgust. I even entertained the idea of going with CJ whenever they left. Not now. Screw that. I'm not destined to be some housewife trapped indoors.

"You're still young," Stacey teases. "Overly independent right now. Don't worry. Your feelings will change once you fall in love."

Doubtful.

"Who knows? With the way CJ looks at you and you back at him, that might be happening sooner rather than later," she says with a knowing smirk. "Let's talk in a year and see if you still feel the same way."

Stacey watches me with a sickly-sweet smile that makes my eye twitch. Something about this woman is weird. She's trying too hard to be nice.

"Okay, well, if you don't need anything else, we'll leave you to it," I say with false cheer. "Come on, baby bro. Let's see what Mommy has for you to eat."

He whines when I snatch him up, but I don't care. I don't like him sitting beside her. She's creepy. If Ryder were here, he'd laugh at me and tell me I'm delusional.

I stalk out of the bedroom, ignoring Dawson's wails. In the hallway, Declan and Kota are playing with both Mage and Spirit, tossing a ball back and forth. I kick the ball away from Kota, laughing when he calls me a buttface.

Mom is in the kitchen with Owen's wife, Tee, Mya, and Seth's wife, Lisa. I thrust the baby at her. "He wants you, Mom."

Mya, picking up on my sass, smothers a laugh. Both Tee and Lisa regard me with wide eyes and raised brows.

Mom motions with her head out of the kitchen as she takes Dawson. She soothes him while following me out of the house and onto the porch.

"Care to explain?" she asks, cutting her eyes over to me. "You're in quite a mood today."

"I'm getting my period," I lie, sneering at her. When you have your period, you're basically allowed to be a bitch.

"No, you're not," Mom says with a heavy sigh. "You're letting that girl get to you."

Mya.

She must always be on her period because she's always a mega bitch.

"I'll be glad when she's gone," I grumble, admitting how much I dislike her.

"It'll be nice to have our home again," Mom agrees, flashing me a conspiratorial grin. "Won't be long."

I shift on my feet, scanning the yard until I can see the gate. Seth was one of the men left behind to guard the homestead. He leans against the gate with his hat pulled down low. The dude is probably sleeping. Some guard he is. I'd be a better watchman than him but no, they desperately need someone to make spaghetti noodles and fold the dry laundry. Gag.

"What's up with that Stacey lady?" I ask, turning from the incompetent man to look at my mother. "She's weird."

Mom purses her lips. "You're sheltered, Rae. Your exposure to people is very limited. There will be people you come across that you don't mesh well with."

"She tries too hard," I argue. "It's like she's been tasked with being my best friend. Did you put her up to this since Mya is such a bitch?"

Mom pops me on the cheek. Not hard enough to bruise, but enough to get my attention. "Language."

I want to call *her* a bitch too, but I bite my tongue. Dawson tries to swat at me, so I give him my evil glare that makes his older brothers cry. He bursts into tears, making me cackle with laughter.

"Just try for me and Daddy," Mom huffs. "Please. It's not forever. All I'm asking is for you to make peace with these people until they leave. Their families have been hit hard with trauma and heartache. The least we can do is be kind to them."

I know this is an argument I'll never win. So for the sake of both our sanities, I nod in agreement. "Yes, ma'am."

She leans in and kisses the cheek she just smacked. "Love you, Rae. You're fiery just like your father. It's a great quality that'll serve you well in life."

I'm gaping after her long after she disappears inside. Since when is my combative nature a great quality? And she literally just smacked me for it. Ugh, parents are confusing.

So are brothers.

My mind drifts to last night before the men left. Ryder pressed himself against me. His mouth was hot against my cheek and so close to my lips. I'd loved the thrill that had zipped through my body. Ryder didn't even kiss me and it was still better than the actual kissing I'd done with CJ. With CJ, it was just motions.

I bet Ryder kisses like he wants to eat you alive.

I bet his cock would love to rub up against me as he shoved his tongue against mine.

My mouth waters at the thought. It's twisted and wrong. Weeks ago I couldn't stop thinking about Ronan doing that very same thing. I'd still give anything to defy all the rules and kiss my older brother, but I can also definitively say the same about Ryder too.

There really is something wrong with me because I'd be happy to kiss them both.

Maybe these women are being strange around me because they can sense the wrongness inside me. Maybe I'm transparent and they know I want things I'm not allowed to have.

Maybe I should leave, all right.

But instead of with CJ's group or to town with Wild and his family, maybe I should just run far, far away where no one knows me.

I can be whoever I want to be.

CHAPTER EIGHTEEN

ronan

M Y MIND IS EVERYWHERE BUT ON THIS HUNT
for Kristen's abusers.

The storm from last night brought cooler
temperatures and saturated the forest through and
through, but the heat that still pools in my gut can't
be put out.

I'm burning from the inside out.

Heat licks at me anytime I catch Ryder's eye as we
silently traipse through the thick underbrush.

He rubbed me through my clothes until I came. My
ultimate fantasy came to life last night as me and my
brother found shelter from the raging storm.

He was jealous.

Somehow he knew I'd kissed Logan and it made
him furious.

To say I was shocked he'd put his hand on my
dick was the understatement of the year. Ryder
expertly rubbed me until I made a mess of my

underwear—underwear that I'd removed in the middle of the night and stuffed deep in my backpack. Having to hunt going commando was worth it.

Last night was the best night of my life.

Kissing Logan wasn't bad either. It was really nice, in fact. I'd wanted his attention and touch so fucking badly.

Until Ryder.

With Ryder, it's different. Between us, we have history and friendship and an unbreakable bond. We're brothers. The feelings go much deeper than the novelty of meeting another man who wanted to kiss and touch me.

It's wrong, though.

He's a man *and* my brother.

I can't even begin to imagine what my parents would think. Or Rae. Rae would feel so betrayed.

Guilt gnaws at my gut, making the meager breakfast of jerky sour in my stomach.

As good as last night felt with Ryder, especially when I could calm him down from being so angry, it can't happen. We're family. It's just not right. And as thrilling as kissing Logan was, that's wrong on a whole other level. He's married. None of these scenarios are good or something to be proud of.

I'm destined to be alone.

My chest aches at the thought of spending my days lonely and without a companion. I may prefer the touch of a man, but if I had to make a choice between no one and a woman, I'd choose a woman.

I want to love and be loved.

I want to have my own family to care for and protect.

Ryder keeps glancing my way, but I avoid his stare. What does he see when he looks at me? A fucked-up brother who's drowning in shame? A young man he must protect from his own actions?

Why can't I just be normal?

My gut churns with disgust. I hate that my brain seems to be wired completely wrong. In all the books I've read, not one of them talks about being in love with your brother and having a sexual relationship with him.

Not. One.

And the magazines Wild slips us?

Men and women together, but it damn sure doesn't speak of them being siblings.

No, all the fantasies and sick, twisted dreams I have are all of my own making. I'm no genius, but I can almost guarantee if my parents knew my desires, this would have the power to destroy my family. They already run a tight ship, making sure to keep our alone times with Raegan at a minimum. The knowledge of what I want to do with their son could be enough to not only fracture our family, but to have them hating me.

I would die if my family hated me or sent me away because of my sick fantasies.

Fantasies I acted on. Fantasies I encouraged to become real by pushing Ryder. Sure, maybe it wasn't exactly intentional, but my actions led us to this moment.

I kissed Logan and let him touch me, and then left Ryder to deal with the aftermath.

I did this.

If my parents send me away, I'll have no one to blame but myself.

The thought of living far removed from those I love with my entire being makes my stomach tighten with unease. Bile creeps up my throat and my head spins.

I wouldn't make it a week without them.

Not that I don't have what it takes to survive, because I absolutely do thanks to Dad's constant teachings. No, I'd die from loneliness.

My heart would crack right down the center, split apart, and I'd bleed out until I was nothing.

All the thoughts inside my head are chaotic and loud despite the near silent trudging of our boots through the underbrush. Occasionally, Rowdy, who's ahead of us, will hold up a fist, meaning for us to stop. He cocks his head, seemingly listening past the chirping birds and whispering wind as if to uncover the true location of Kristen's assailants, only to lower his hand back down and continue his trek.

Before I'm once again caught up in my mental trap where I'm bouncing back and forth between berating myself or imagining a horrible life alone, I hear it.

Voices.

Hushed but frequent.

Then we hear a laugh.

Rowdy unslings the rifle off his shoulder and holds

it at the ready. Ryder and I both carry knives that we've unsheathed as we prowl toward the sounds of men.

"…fourteen or not, I still want to tap that."

I immediately recognize Jace's voice. CJ smothers a laugh, but it's still loud enough to scare away a bird. Rowdy points to a clearing up ahead. The two guys are sitting on a log, a plume of smoke between them. I recognize the smell as marijuana. Wild's smuggled a joint out here a time or two and convinced us to smoke with him.

"Who says she'd even be into you?" CJ asks, passing him the blunt.

I'm wondering why we haven't alerted ourselves to the men yet. Rowdy has rocked to a halt, slightly lowered as he listens.

"Lack of options, man," Jace says with a snigger. "Have you seen her choices?"

"She certainly can't," CJ tosses back. "I guess it would be good for your ass to be fucking a blind chick."

Destiny?

They're talking about *our* fourteen-year-old sister?

Where Ryder and I tense with realization, Rowdy is already tearing toward the duo. I'm frozen in place, wondering if he's going to blow both their heads off.

Crack!

I suck in a sharp breath as I watch CJ collapse onto the forest floor after having been smacked in the head by the butt of Rowdy's rifle. Jace, shocked by the surprise attack, scrambles away and stumbles over his own feet. Ryder and I rush forward—to do what, I'm not sure.

Rowdy snags Jace by his flannel shirt and shoves him up against a tree. His rifle falls to the ground and he produces a wicked-sharp knife he got while visiting Uncle Atticus during the time that changed Rowdy—a knife that could end this pervert with one well-delivered jab.

"You even look at my little sister and I will carve your eyeballs out," Rowdy snarls. "If you touch her, I'll carve them out and make your dipshit cousin eat them."

"Dude," Jace grinds out. "We were just fucking around and being stupid. No one really wants to fuck her."

Rowdy digs the blade into Jace's flesh just below his jawline, piercing the skin and producing a dark red rivulet of blood that races down his flesh. "Stop talking or I'll cut your fucking tongue out too."

He's going to kill him.

CJ groans from the ground. Rowdy tenses but leaves his back to him, choosing to focus on the threat in front of him. Because we're family and have his back, me and Ryder step near CJ, making sure he doesn't rush our brother or some shit.

"I'm sorry," Jace mutters. "Man, I really am sorry. It was unacceptable. I get that."

Rowdy tilts his head to the side, the tension in his shoulders and back never leaving. "I don't believe you and I don't fucking trust you."

Once I make sure Ryder has a watchful eye on CJ, I slowly creep toward our older brother. When Jace sees me, relief flashes in his eyes. It unnerves me that he sees me as his savior. He was just talking shit about fucking our baby sister and thinks I'm going to save him.

Because he can sense I have some weird thing going on with Logan?

Am I that transparent?

What he doesn't see is my unwavering desire to protect my family. Not his. Mine.

"You can't kill him," I say, gently touching Rowdy on the back. "But you can kick his ass. That shit he deserves."

Jace's eyes narrow to slits and something dark passes over his expression. Before I can interpret it, Rowdy releases him. Briefly. In the next second, his knife is tossed away and he's charging Jace.

"Oof!" Jace grunts as Rowdy sacks him.

Rowdy, now straddling his adversary, raises his fist and then slams it down on Jace's face. I shy away from the brutality, choosing to look back at Ryder. Ryder smirks, his boot firmly planted on CJ's spine, keeping him sprawled out on the earth.

Crack! Crack! Crack!

Rowdy is relentless in putting the beat down on Jace. Just because I don't want to watch him bloody him to a pulp doesn't mean I don't agree with it. It would have been different if Jace were talking shit about Raegan.

That girl can handle herself and could probably give him a similar ass whipping that Rowdy's doling out.

But Dez?

Destiny is innocent and fragile. She's a sweetheart who deserves to be loved and protected. Not lusted after by men who have no business saying such things.

Yeah, Jace has earned every punch.

"He's going to murder him," Ryder says in a conversational tone. "Shame."

The sarcasm in his voice has me breaking into a highly inappropriate grin. I bite down on my lip to make it go away. Ryder's attention falls to my mouth, which in turn has heat prickling over my flesh.

Last night was supposed to be a one-time thing.

I'm supposed to be doing everything I can not to think about Ryder and what we did when we were all alone.

My dick, no longer trapped by my cotton boxers, twitches and swells, nudging against the zipper of my jeans.

Seriously?

I'm getting hard right now?

With three other witnesses, two of which are on the fast track to becoming enemies?

Unbelievable.

Ryder's smile widens, a knowing glint in his eyes. That taunting, teasing expression he wears is not helpful. Not helpful at all.

"When you're done with that shithead," Ryder calls

out to Rowdy, "do you want to take a few swings at this one?"

Right.

There's a squirming man under my brother's boot.

It's not just me and Ryder, alone and flirting. These shared smiles are definitely some strange way of flirting. Fuck.

Rowdy lets loose a violent roar and then slings himself off Jace's prone body. He staggers to his feet before scooping up his weapons. Jace, face bruised and smeared with blood, moans in pain. He tenderly touches his cheek and whimpers.

He's alive, but that shit has to hurt.

Ryder finally releases CJ and steps away from him. CJ rises to his feet, shoots me a disgusted glare, and then rushes over to his cousin. Rowdy is busy shouldering his rifle and sheathing his knife, seemingly no longer bothered by Jace aside from the crimson rage still painting his cheeks. His chest heaves and his hair drips with sweat. Other than those tells, he ignores the moaning piece of shit on the ground.

"Let's get something straight," Rowdy says, voice deceptively calm as he turns to regard CJ and Jace. "You fell, had a fight with a bear, or ran into a fucking tree. I don't give a shit what you tell them, but you won't tell them it was me."

Jace, whose face is swelling heavily on his left side, doesn't say anything but instead glowers at my older brother through his one eye that's not swollen shut.

"If you tell them it was me," Rowdy continues, "I'll tell my father what you want to do to his child." Rowdy lets loose a dark chuckle. "What you just received will feel like a favor. My father won't be so generous. Understood?"

Both CJ and Jace each nod once.

"Good." Rowdy motions for me and Ryder to follow him. "Let's get the hell away from these assholes."

CHAPTER NINETEEN

ryder

I CAN'T EXPLAIN WHAT HAPPENED LAST NIGHT.

It was terrible and beautiful rolled into one confusing memory.

The flames from my jealous anger at Ronan kissing Logan lashed at my mind, singeing it irreparably. I wanted to burn Logan's touch, scent, and presence from Ronan's flesh.

This morning, I woke up right where I'd fallen asleep. Arm slung possessively around my brother. Cock hard and aching for some kind of forbidden release I don't dare to think of.

His lips were slightly parted as he slept, punching me in the gut with the overwhelming urge to kiss him again.

I refrained.

Barely.

Ever since, we've been carefully avoiding each other's stare and proximity.

That is, except when I had my boot smashing that

cockroach, CJ. In that frozen sliver of time, Ronan's nostrils flared, his eyes warmed with heat, and he ran his perfect tongue over his bottom lip. We had a moment, and it was dangerous. Dangerous because I wanted to forget anyone and everyone so that I could tackle my older brother to the ground.

I wanted to consume him with my mouth in every possible way.

Hell, I still want to.

But with Dad and the others rejoining us, I have to be more careful than ever.

"There's no trail," Dad grunts, passing me a packet of nuts to munch on. "Which is…*strange*."

"You think they're going to come back?" I focus on my father's furrowed brow, carefully avoiding his eyes. "You know, like when we sleep again or something?"

Dad doesn't speak right away, choosing instead to flick his gaze over everyone in camp. CJ and Jace are here, with the latter looking worse for wear considering Rowdy's beat down on him. Thankfully, fuck face Logan stays near his brother rather than by mine. Ronan and Rowdy have been scanning the woods nearby, looking for dry sticks and brush for kindling.

"I think…" Dad sighs and cuts his eyes my way. "I think something doesn't add up."

When he turns his head again, attention landing on CJ and Jace, my stomach tightens. I clench my teeth together, hoping not to give away my knowledge of what really happened to Jace's ugly face. Earlier, when everyone met up again, Jace and CJ wove a convincing tale that they'd been attacked by the very two men who we were looking for.

"Dad, I…" I start, ready to cave and admit it was Rowdy who doled out the much-deserved ass kicking, but words fail me.

Ronan and Rowdy choose that moment to return, arms laden with sticks, saving me from my guilty conscience. I jump to my feet, rushing over to help them with the fire starting.

Dad's gaze is sharp as he watches us. My father is not one to be lied to or deceived. None of us kids are able to get away with it, which is why it's better to avoid him when he's in tracker mode.

If Dad finds out we're in on CJ and Jace's lie, we'll be in a shit ton of trouble. Last time someone got into big trouble, they got sent away to Uncle Atticus and came back changed. And not in a good way.

Looking at you, Rowdy…

The very thought of being so far removed from Ronan and Raegan and the rest of my family has my heart rate speeding up. It would be fucking horrible and lonely. There's no way in hell I'd ever willingly do that, which means I need to get my game face on so Dad doesn't sniff out the lie.

Twinkling stars can be seen peeking between the cover

of the trees above us. We're miles from home, camped out, and disappointed. Us finding the perpetrators feels like a fool's errand, impossible and out of reach.

Everyone is sitting around our now-roaring fire, voices low and sparse. The overall feeling I'm picking up from the camp as a whole is defeat. Those bastards came into our home, hurt a defenseless woman, and are still out there. Even with so many of us, we've yet to find them.

"…bringing people into our fold to avoid inbreeding," Michael murmurs to my dad. "It's common through these parts and we don't want to become some statistic. We're growing something here. A community."

Dad nods at Michael before burning his stare into me. With one penetrating look, I feel exposed. It's as though he can see the lie of what happened to CJ and Jace, the memory of Raegan's body hot against mine, the tingling sensation of my hand as I remember what I did with it against Ronan's dick.

I'm guilty.

There's no hiding from it.

"What are your plans?" Owen asks. "To make sure your children don't…*you know.*"

Dad flinches at his words, imperceptibly so, but I notice. "We have people in town. Our kids are welcome to experience a taste of city life when they're able to. Your concerns aren't any of ours."

Now Dad's the one lying. Not that we can't go to Uncle Atticus's. No, he's lying about the lack of concern.

If he wasn't worried to some degree, he and Mom wouldn't lose their fucking minds anytime me or Ronan are alone with Raegan. Our most recent family feud was over this very subject. Awkward and humiliating.

The conversation doesn't die, of course. Owen and Michael keep beating the fear into Dad's head. With each passing moment, his body grows more tense and I can practically feel the waves of worry rippling from him.

"Out here, in the wild, birth defects are a real concern. And if any of your boys make the mistake of fucking one of your girls, that concern is going to become a reality," Owen says, casually glancing my way. "It'd come out fucked-up and you'd be forced to put that abomination down."

Abomination.

My gut recoils, a mixture of shock and indignation.

"That can't really happen," I blurt out, unable to stop myself. "Right?"

Dad stiffens and Owen gives me a patronizing smile.

"Ryder," Ronan mutters, shooting me a pleading look to stop talking.

But I can't.

"Dad, tell them that can't happen." My voice is hoarse as I briefly imagine Raegan pregnant. The thought of her delivering a baby that has to be *put down* makes me physically sick to my stomach. "Dad… We wouldn't kill a baby even if it was a little messed up. Right?"

"You've seen Eve's gravestones," Rowdy answers, not meeting my stare. "From…"

Her past. Her sick, fucked-up past.

Dad told us the story of how Aunt Eve's babies died. She kept getting pregnant when her brothers and dad would rape her.

They were *abominations* and had died because of it.

Or were they *put down*?

I'm going to throw up.

Fuck.

Jerking to my feet, I spit out an excuse that I need to take a piss. Truth is, I need to escape. I need to run far away from the pitying stares and haunting thoughts of something horrible happening to Raegan.

Mom and Dad's fears of us being alone with her aren't made up. They're afraid for us because of what awful could come from it if we were to sleep with our sister.

Branches whip angrily at me, lashing at my face and tearing at my hair as I punch my way through the forest blindly in the total darkness. My charging thoughts fuel me and I keep stomping away, away, away until I can no longer see the orange glow from the fire or hear the voices of the other men.

Silence.

I lean my back against a thick tree, chest heaving with exertion. Slowly, I drag myself down until I'm sitting on my ass on the hard, exposed roots. My back burns from the bark scraping my flesh through my flannel. Hot tears burn at my eyes, but I refuse to let them fall.

Why am I so upset?

Because, deep down, you thought you could have her. And you can't.

Having her means hurting everyone around me, including any future babies.

My throat constricts and I gag. Nothing comes up, thankfully, and I swallow back down the bitterness at the back of my tongue.

An ache has formed deep in the cavity of my chest. I absently rub at my diaphragm in an attempt to ease the hurt.

Raegan is completely off-limits. The end. No negotiation. She's a dream that must stay locked away in my mind, trapped forever to remain safe from me.

What about Ronan?

He can't get pregnant…

The thought gets shoved into the same place Raegan has gone to in my mind. Just because he can't get pregnant doesn't mean a sexual relationship with him, beyond the "mistake" that happened last night, couldn't hurt our family beyond fixing.

I don't want to hurt anyone.

Especially not Raegan or Ronan.

I want them both to be happy and loved and protected.

I'll be damned if I'm the one who fucks everything up for this family.

Crack.

The sound of a stick breaking nearby has me freezing and cocking my head to listen. It could be an animal or those bastards we're hunting. Or it could be Ronan come to cheer me up. My heart squeezes at the thought of him giving me one of his comforting hugs.

"You okay, Ry?"

Dad's gruff voice cuts through all thoughts of Ronan and hits me right in the stomach. It's like my mind is muddled with all these wrong, confusing things bouncing around and now they've spilled free for all to see. Dad, perceptive to a fault, is probably picking them all up, inspecting each one and figuring out how to proceed.

"Ryder."

"I'm fine," I croak out.

I'm not fine. I'm so completely screwed up in the head and I don't know how to fix it. I don't know how to erase how I've been feeling lately. To undo the trouble my dick keeps getting me into.

Dad crunches softly through the brush and then sits down close enough to me I can smell his familiar earthy scent. His sigh is heavy and sad.

I bury my face in my palms, dreading whatever talk we're about to have. Whether it's comfort or solutions, either way the conversation is going to be uncomfortable.

"I've been thinking about it a lot lately and when Atticus comes for his visit, I want you to go back with them. Get a taste of town life for a bit. Maybe find a girl worth settling down for."

No comfort. Solutions.

"Dad," I murmur. "I don't want to. I want to stay here."

He sucks in a deep breath before exhaling his words. "It's not a request, Ryder."

Not a request.

The finality in his words is a punch to the gut. It knocks the breath right out of me. My lungs ache from lack of oxygen, making me grow dizzy.

This can't be real.

I'm being exiled. Just like that. Without even acting on anything with Raegan, but for simply thinking it. I gulp in a gasp of air and attempt to find my words again.

"Ronan will hate town life," I argue, voice growing shrill with panic. "You saw what it did to Rowdy. I can handle it, but Ronan can't. He needs you guys."

I need you guys.

I choke back a sob that threatens. Hysteria is sucking me into its void, drowning me mercilessly.

"Ronan's not going." Dad's words are clipped and final. "Just you, Son."

Quiet rushes in around us, growing deafening with each passing second. Just me. Not me and Ronan? Does he know about Ronan preferring men?

"That's not fair," I blurt out. "Why just me?"

I'll be damned if I out Ronan about his sexuality, but I also can't lie down and take this injustice.

"Ronan's different as you've said. I don't have to worry about him." He pauses, letting that sink in before continuing in a gruff voice. "He's not the one who needs the exposure to new people."

"Dad, please." My bottom lip wobbles and I'm thankful for the darkness so he can't see the edge of an emotional breakdown. "Dad…"

"I understand this hurts. You're so close to your siblings. This isn't forever, Ryder. This is for now. You come back to us when you're ready."

After you find a woman who isn't your sister.

That's the part he leaves off but is heavily implied.

"What if I come back ruined like Rowdy?" I ask, voice cracking.

"He's not ruined," Dad growls as he stands. His hand clamps down on my shoulder and he squeezes. "There's nothing wrong with your brother. He's just no longer naive to the world. You, my son, still have so much to learn. Take this opportunity and use it well."

He releases me and then leaves me alone with my misery.

My pain is covered in shame like the wetness of the forest—saturating every part of it, even down to the buried roots. There's no hiding from it.

I'm being banished.

Robbed of happiness and love.

I'll come back ruined.

If I ever come back.

CHAPTER TWENTY

raegan

A RUMBLE, LOUD ENOUGH TO MAKE THE windows rattle in the big house, tugs me from my ultimate boredom of folding laundry. I abandon the pile of towels to rush out the door. There are people everywhere—just not my favorite people.

Ronan and Ryder and Dad are still gone.

The deep, grumbly sounds are vibrations from music and an engine. Someone's coming.

Racing across our yard, I steer clear of Mya, though we both manage to flash each other the bitchiest glares we can muster. The guy on guard duty is frowning my way but hasn't left the safety of the closed gate. I rush past him, flinging myself out of the protection of our home and into the wilderness beyond it. Ignoring the man who calls after me, I hoof it to the edge of the fence and onto the road to wait, hands on my hips as I squint at the road.

The vibrations and rhythmic beat of bass grow

closer and closer until a metal beast rounds the bend. I recognize the obnoxious truck—all shiny chrome, sleek black paint, and tires every bit as tall as me.

Wild.

Wild Knox, my betrothed.

Not really, but if our parents had it their way, we'd have fallen in love the second we laid eyes on each other.

Love is the furthest thing from either of our minds.

Yet, I still wait eagerly for his annoying ass to arrive. I need normalcy, and with Wild, I can guarantee he'll be his usual antagonistic self, which for once is welcomed.

Anything to stop thinking about our visitors and the drama they've brought with them.

I wait in the middle of the dirt road, nearly over-grown with brush, as Wild's truck becomes clearer in the distance. The engine roars as he speeds up. I know he can see me, which is why we're now engaged in a game of chicken.

Me against his massive metal beast.

Standing my ground, I lift one hand from my hip, thrusting it into the air in front of me to wave my mid-dle finger at him. It's my usual welcoming gesture when-ever I see him. He responds by gassing it, no doubt taunting me to move.

At this point, I'd almost be thankful for him to put me out of my misery.

Flatten me like a pancake.

He'd get his ass whipped so bad by both our dads.

I remain rooted in place, not wavering despite the

speed at which he's approaching. My heart leaps into my throat and it takes everything in me not to move. The truck grows larger and louder with each passing second.

And then he's yards away, laying on the horn.

Asshole.

At the last second, he jerks the wheel to the left and slams on the brakes. Air swishes past me, sending my hair flinging in my face. I swear I felt his side mirror graze over the material of my shirt covering my arm. Whirling around, I follow to where he's skidded to a stop, truck parked crooked and taking up the road.

The passenger door opens and some guy around my age climbs out. He's tall with shaggy blond hair and is wearing sunglasses.

"Holy shit," he says in greeting. "You almost got killed. You do know this idiot is driving and no one is safe on the roads, especially not hot chicks running through the woods."

I narrow my eyes. "I wasn't running through the woods. I was standing on my property. Who are you again? Don't tell me you're actually friends with that fucker."

He snorts, offering me his hand. "That fucker is my best friend. I'm Chet."

"Funny," I snip, eyeing his hand warily. "He never mentioned you."

"Well, he sure as hell mentioned you," Chet says with a wicked grin. "Said you're his future wifey or some shit."

The rear door opens on the passenger side and another kid around my age gracefully leaps out. She, too, has blond hair, but hers is silky and sleek. Her cropped top and short denim shorts that reveal long, tanned legs make her seem more worldly than me, though. My plain jeans and T-shirt feel boring and drab in comparison.

"Hi," the girl says, wearing a bright smile. "I'm Sadie. Chet's sister."

As interesting as these two people I've never met are, I'm antsy to speak to him. Stupid Wild. Operator of the dumb truck that makes too much noise. Not that I miss him or anything. I just need something…normal. Fighting with Wild is something I'm one hundred percent comfortable with.

The two golden-haired teens watch me with unhidden interest like I'm a specimen they're here to study. Another truck door slams shut. Seconds later, Wild saunters around the truck.

He's beautiful.

No one and I mean no one can deny that, not even me.

It's just his mind is a mess. He's calculating and mean and crude. Wild is the exact opposite of everything good my brothers are.

Wild has a ball cap pulled low over his brow and his head is dipped slightly, so all I can see is the cruel slant of his full lips. My hackles rise and I fist my hands, steeling myself for whatever barb he has ready for me.

"Sorry," Wild rumbles in a deeper voice than I last

remember. His tone is far from sorry. "I didn't see you there."

I roll my eyes and ignore his apology. "Where's the rest of your family?"

"Twins are sick," he says, annoyance dripping from his words. "Again. What else is new? They'll be here in a few days."

Sadie and Chet remain frozen like beautiful statues, their shiny gold-spun hair the only thing moving as the wind dances by us. Their matching smiles give me the creeps.

Wild slowly approaches until he's towering over me. He's bigger than my brothers. Wider through the shoulders and packing more muscle. The older he gets, the more he looks like a spitting image of Uncle Atticus—minus the man bun and beard and tattoos. His slightly unhinged green-eyed glare reminds me of Aunt Eve, though.

"Looking frumpier than usual, wifey," Wild says, bearing a wolfish grin. "It's like you don't even try for me anymore. You wound me."

I plant my hands on his solid, massive chest and shove him. He stumbles back a step before roaring with laughter. His weird friends join in, politely trying to muffle their amusement.

"Don't be a dick." I cross my arms over my chest and glower at him. "There's enough of those around lately."

And, as if on cue, dick number one appears.

"New people!" Mya squeals, running over to us. "Hi, I'm Mya. Raegan's bestie."

I snap my head toward her and curl my lip up in disgust. We are not besties.

"Holy shit," Wild says with a chuckle. "Your dad let people onto his backwoods inbreeding factory?"

I'm going to kill him one day.

Just pick up a rock and smash it against his mouth that says mean things endlessly. Maybe if his teeth were hanging from the roots, he'd have a harder time spitting out his nonsense.

"Wild Knox," Wild greets, turning on his fake charm for Mya. "These are my friends Sadie and Chet."

Mya shakes Wild's hand and is slow to release it.

"Girlfriend?" Mya boldly asks, eyeing Sadie with a forced smile.

Wild chuckles. "Nah. Didn't you hear? I'm gonna marry that girl right there."

Me. I'm that girl.

Fat fucking chance.

Mya takes her time scrutinizing me as she steps closer to Wild. "What a catch."

They all crack up laughing at my expense. I'm half tempted to whip my knife out. Maybe I'd stop being a joke at that point. And, if that didn't work, I could just poke them a few times with the blade.

"I brought gifts," Wild says once his chuckles have subsided. "Do you like Skittles, Mya?"

My mouth waters for those colorful candies, but I

don't dare let Wild or Mya see any emotion on my face. Wild never brings me gifts. He knows the things I like and purposefully gives them to my siblings instead. He's a little—*all six-feet-plus of him*—asshole. Luckily, Uncle Atticus always pulls through for me.

I miss Ronan.

He always runs interference between me and Wild. Ronan, who actually likes Wild as a friend, somehow manages to diffuse the situation whenever he's here. My heart aches to see him.

Could I confess to him the crazy, charged moment I shared with Ryder?

Would he care? Be pissed off? Want to claim me instead?

Heat burns deep in my gut, momentarily distracting me from being the oddball out of this group of beautiful jerks. I catch snippets of Mya explaining who she is, why they're here, and where the rest of the camp went.

"Seriously, dude, your truck just woke up the entire state of Alaska."

I know that voice.

Ronan.

A happy squeal erupts from me as I chase down the voice. Emerging from the woods are Ronan and Ryder. I take off running, ignoring the watchful stares of Wild and his crew. Ronan is ready for me, arms spread wide and waiting.

"You're back!" I leap into his arms, hooking my legs

around his waist and nearly tackling him with my momentum. "Oh my God, I missed you so much!"

Ronan laughs, hugging me back. "Missed you too, Rae."

I playfully smack wet kisses all over his face until he groans, shoving me away from him. Once he manages to completely pluck me off him, I turn to Ryder, still grinning stupidly. His brow is furrowed, and his pouty lips are pressed together in a firm line.

"I missed both of you," I say, this time leaning into Ryder for a hug. "So much."

We're not typically the huggers, but things are different between us lately. He's stiff and bristly acting, but a second later, his large palm finds my hip, burning me through my layers of clothes. Both he and Ronan are a bit rank, smelling like they spent the past couple of days not bothering to bathe. I don't care, though. Their sweaty, woodsy scent is still better than Wild's fancy cologne he wears that is nauseating.

"Should I be jealous, wifey dearest?" Wild asks, the cruel edge of his voice cutting right through me.

His insinuation pisses me off, probably because it's a little too close to the truth.

Ronan starts to say something, no doubt ready to calm me down, but I move like lightning. Jerking myself out of Ryder's hug, I fly toward Wild. Since he's not expecting me, I get the element of surprise. With a leap when I'm close enough to see his stupid, handsome face, I swing my fist, aiming right for it.

Crack!

Wild's head jerks hard to his right and his ball cap gets flung to the earth. He whips his head back to me and fingers his lip that trickles blood. I'm pretty sure I hit his jaw based on the way my hand now throbs like hell, but it appears he bit his lip from the impact of my hit.

"You bitch," Wild snarls, swiping at the blood with his fingers and staring at them in disbelief. "You hit me."

"Keep running your mouth and I'll kick you in the balls next time," I threaten, baring my teeth at him. "Test me, asshole. Go on."

Ronan grabs the wrist of my hand that hurts so bad I wonder if I broke a finger or two. "Come on, killer. Let's get out of here and catch up."

My other hand, uninjured, is quite capable of offering Wild another display of my middle finger. I take satisfaction in the crazed, angry glare he shoots my way.

God, that felt good.

Even if Mom tears me a new one for being violent.

It was worth it.

CHAPTER TWENTY-ONE

ronan

RAEGAN FOLLOWS STUBBORNLY BEHIND ME. SHE'S pissed at Wild, but what else is new?

Oh, that's right. Punching him is new.

She's going to get into so much shit over this.

I'd actually looked forward to hanging out with Wild and the people he brought with him, but Raegan's more important. She always comes first.

Does that put Ryder second?

My heart lurches in my chest. Thoughts of the other night, his hand stroking me off and his mouth on mine, assault me like hail in a vicious storm. Each memory is bruising.

I had a sexual encounter with my brother.

It appeared we'd squashed it and were both doing a great job of keeping our minds off it when we'd over-heard Jace and CJ trash-talking Destiny. Somehow, during that moment, flames of lust ignited once more with a few stolen glances.

And then…

Then things got weird.

Ryder was yelling at Michael and Owen and Dad. He was damn near panicking about incest that led to him running off. I'd been poised to go after him despite the judging stares of our visitors, but Dad beat us to the punch.

Whatever Dad said to Ryder broke him.

He hasn't spoken a word of real substance to me since. I've been dying to get him alone, to force him to look at me, and demand he spill whatever Dad said to him.

Is he in trouble?

"Ryder was quiet," Raegan says as we enter the gate of our property and head toward my cabin. "Did you guys catch the bad men?"

My stomach tightens knowing those monsters got away. "No. They're still out there, but Dad thinks we ran them off."

When we reach the cabin, I notice Destiny isn't inside, which means she's probably helping Mom at the big house. I'm glad Raegan and I will be awarded this rare moment of privacy now that our property is overrun by people. I guide her over to the bed and we crawl into our usual spots. She smells like strawberries and I smell like ass.

Despite me desperately needing a shower or a quick dunk in the river, she snuggles against me, splaying her punching hand on my chest. Avoiding her gaze, I pick it up, inspecting it for serious injuries. She whines and groans when I push and prod, but it's evident nothing is broken.

"You could have broken your hand," I chide, bringing her middle knuckle to my mouth and kissing it.

She huffs, her breath tickling over my chest. "I wish I had broken his face."

"The great Wild Knox was bleeding," I tease, chuckling. "I'd say you achieved your goal."

A cute giggle escapes her and I squeeze her to me.

"You smell like dirty underwear," Raegan says, plucking at my shirt.

"And to think I'm not even wearing underwear."

She stiffens and then pops up on one elbow. "What?"

Heat floods my cheeks and I feel like an idiot for blurting that out. What happened between me and Ryder was both horrible and amazing. Keeping it bottled in damn near hurts.

"Ro," she grumbles. "Tell me. Did you…you know…with Logan?"

The goofy smile on my lips pulls into a quick frown. "Uhhh…"

"Out with it. I need to know every detail. You dirty dog!"

I close my eyes for a moment, trying to remember the kiss I shared with Logan. It feels like eons ago. Later that night with Ryder was more potent and raw, coating my every cell with blissful memory.

I have to tell her.

"If I tell you something, you have to promise not to tell a soul. You can't even tell Ryder I told you," I whisper, nervous energy skittering its way through my veins. "Promise, Rae. Not even when you're pissed and you want to get a rise out of Mom and Dad."

Her brows scrunch together and her eyes dart back and forth as she studies me. "Okay. Should I be scared? You sound serious."

"I am serious. If you told anyone…" I trail off and bite down onto my bottom lip. "You just can't."

"I promise," she vows. "Now tell me."

Apprehension flickers in her eyes, making me re-think everything. What me and Ryder did alone in the tent in the dark probably shouldn't ever make its way to the light of day. And yet…

I want to talk about it.

I want to remember.

I want it to be real.

Closing my eyes, I avoid my sister's stare and blurt out the words. "Ryder, uh, got me off."

"Off what?" Confusion laces her tone.

Snapping my eyes back open, I frown at her. "Like made me come."

"Made you come," she says slowly and then her cheeks blaze crimson. "You had sex with our brother?"

"W-What?" I shriek, *yes, shriek*, and cover her mouth with my hand despite mine being the loud one. "It wasn't like that."

She shoves my hand away.

"Wasn't like what? Tell me, Ro. You're not making any sense."

I groan, rolling until I'm half on top of her so I can meet her gaze. "You know how Ryder gets hard for you sometimes?"

She blushes again and nods.

"I do the same for him. It just happened, okay? He didn't want Logan touching me, so he took care of my, uh, needs."

"You were hard for him," she breathes, shifting slightly. "And you're hard now."

Hard now?

Holy fuck.

I am.

Because I was remembering every detail of Ryder's hand pressed against my dick through my denim. Not because of Raegan. That's just… *No.*

Her eyelashes flutter and her lips part. I'm suddenly aware of what she must be thinking. That I must want her in the same way I wanted him.

Fuck. Fuck. Fuck.

This is unraveling fast and going to ruin everything.

Why did I have to open my big mouth?

"I love you, Raegan, but I told you. I like…" Men. Guys. Whatever. Just not females, especially not my sister. Not sexually at least.

She flinches, the unspoken words whipping at her. "Got it."

I know I've hurt her because her usually fierce eyes

are glassy with unshed tears. I'm an asshole, but I don't want her to think things that aren't real.

"Get off me," she hisses, spittle hitting me in the face.

As though I've been struck, I jolt away from her, covering my stupid half-hard dick with my hand. Her throat bobs as she swallows down her emotion, eyes darting to the way I try to hide from her.

"So that's it now?" Her voice is shrill as she staggers away. "You two get to be lovers and I'm all alone? I thought you were my best friend!"

I follow after her, unable to get my tongue to work correctly and say the right words. Everything in my head sounds wrong. Anything I say will only hurt her.

"I'm sorry," I mutter. "Whatever you're thinking, it's not like that. The thing that happened was a mistake."

It didn't feel like one.

In that moment, it felt so right.

"A mistake?" She shakes her head and angrily swipes at a rogue tear. "Try telling your face that."

With those words, she storms out of the cabin, leaving my mind an even bigger mess than before.

I'm really fucking everything up and I don't know how to stop it.

Chet's hilarious. I can see why Wild likes him. Sadie is cool too, though she's long since retired to my cabin to bunk with the girls. Now that it's just us guys—me, Ryder, Wild, and Chet—Wild unearths his real gifts to us. The gifts he hid away in his bag until this moment.

Condoms. Lube. Some strange sex toys. Magazines. And alcohol. Always alcohol when Wild's involved.

"That girl, Mya, totally wants to fuck you, Ry," Wild says, grinning wide. "You'll need those condoms so you don't knock her up. It's doubtful any of these women around here even know what birth control is."

Ryder continues strumming on his guitar, ignoring Wild.

Chet snorts out a laugh. "This is some backwoods redneck shit right here. How do you people even survive without like, I don't know, TV or internet or fuckin' Ben & Jerry's?"

"What the hell is Ben & Jerry's?" I ask absently as I thumb through the glossy magazine full of tits, tits, and more tits.

Chet howls with more laughter even though I have no idea why. "That's what I'm talking about, dude! You guys have no idea what you're missing out on. No idea."

"It's not that great having Mya want me. And I'm not missing out on shit. I actually like it here," Ryder grumbles as he sets his guitar aside. He snags a bottle of liquor from Wild, unscrews the cap, and takes a long pull. Then he shudders and damn near gags. "That's fucking terrible."

"But you need pussy, man. I'd die if I lived out here isolated from the female population. There are like a million hot chicks at our school. Hell, half of them take turns spending the night at our house with Sadie," Chet says, reaching for the liquor bottle. "Revolving door of walking blow jobs."

"You get blow jobs from all your sister's friends?" I lift my brows in shock. "How many blow jobs have you had?"

Chet's grin is wolfish. "A helluva lot more than you, my friend."

I tear my gaze from his, focusing on the magazine. The women are scarily perfect. No scars or freckles or blotchy red skin like Raegan's gets when she's angry. Just smooth flesh in varying shades of creams, tans, browns, and black. All of their tits are big too. Some of the women have tattoos on their soft, toned stomachs or slim thighs. Others have metal piercings dangling from their nipples. I wonder what their assholes look like.

One of the pages flips out and a woman uses a toy, pushing it inside her glistening slit. I try to imagine my dick inside her. Would it be hot and slick? Would it strangle me like my hand regularly does?

"You can jerk off later," Wild says, snatching the magazine from me. "I think we need to go fuck with those assholes."

Apparently, Ryder filled Wild and Chet in on everything. Well, not everything. Not what happened with me and him, but everything about the new people, the dipshits CJ and Jace, and our hunting trip where we tried to find the men who hurt Kristen. He's been itching to antagonize and accelerate the situation ever since.

I, for one, am completely happy with hiding away from all of them—Raegan included—while getting drunk and looking at porn mags.

Ryder sits up and drinks more of the liquor before nodding. "I'm game for beating the shit out of CJ. He deserves an ass beating."

"Nah, I'm good," I mutter. "Have fun without me."

Ryder is already on his feet, ignoring my comment. He's juiced and ready for some violence. Wild always brings out the best in him. Not.

I expect Ryder to give me shit for not going, but he pretends I'm not even here or like I never spoke a word. He's being strange and it hurts, but I know he can't stay mad forever. We'll work it out. We always do.

The three of them slip out of the cabin and into the night. I enjoy the quiet, rummaging through Wild's bag to see if it has any other surprises. There are lots of snacks, so I help myself to some chips and then settle in for some more female body studying. For once I'd love for him to bring me something with men only in it. Just fucking once.

Rap. Rap. Rap.

The soft knocking on Ryder's cabin door has me jolting. Quickly, I throw a blanket over the magazines and liquor in case it's Mom or Dad. I open the door, half expecting half hoping for Raegan, but instead am shocked to see Logan.

Handsome, manly, married Logan.

"Hey," he says, flashing me one of his secretive smiles. It's a smile that days ago I'd have nutted in my pants over. Now, it just makes me feel guilty.

"Hey." I shove my hands into my jeans pockets and lift a brow. "What's up?"

"Can we talk?"

I bark out a nervous laugh. "I thought that's what we were doing."

He smirks. "Smartass. Can I come in?"

Being alone with Logan sounds like a terrible idea. I quickly shake my head, ignoring the flash of disappointment in his eyes.

"My brother will be back anytime," I lie. "Better not."

He studies me for a beat, eyes narrowed, but finally nods. My heart trips over itself when he steps nearer, coming to stand just inches away from me. Logan is hot, but things are messy right now. My head is all over the place. I'm not necessarily interested in whatever *this* is.

"The other night," he says softly. "It was—"

"A mistake," I agree. "I know. I'm sorry."

Logan's features harden. "I was going to say hot, Ronan."

"Oh." I pluck my glasses off my face and scrub my palm over it. "Sorry."

"You keep saying that."

When I put my glasses back on, he's even closer than before, watching me with a ravenous stare. He leans in, lips slightly parted, and I turn my head. His warm mouth brushes over my scruffy cheek. An awkward silence fills the air for a long second and then he retreats a few steps.

"You're hot and then cold," he clips out. "It's confusing, man."

He's confused?

I'm the one confused. I've barely come to terms with my feelings for the opposite sex and was crushing on a much older, married man but then got dirty with my brother.

I am definitely the confused one here.

Regret sloshes in my belly, souring the liquor I'd consumed earlier. The urge to throw up is strong. I open my mouth to apologize again, but he waves me off with a sharp cut of his hand through the air.

"I get it. Good night, Ronan."

His words are abrupt and final. A closed door. A period at the end of a sentence. Done. Over.

Logan swivels around and then storms off into the dark night. He's pissed. And that hurts.

Because of the weirdness happening with me and Ryder, I've pushed away an opportunity to be with a man. A real opportunity that could have ended blissfully.

Now, I stand here alone.

I'll always be alone because I certainly can't be with my brother.

CHAPTER TWENTY-TWO

ryder

'M BUZZED, BOTH FROM THE ALCOHOL WILD brought and the anticipation of putting my fist through CJ's teeth. I'll get in trouble, but what does it matter. Dad made his decision. I'm leaving. And soon.

Wild grins over his shoulder at me, the moonlight lighting up his green eyes reminding me of a hungry wolf. He's starved for the violence—to cause trouble and antagonize. Usually, it's Raegan or Rowdy he saves his energy for, but tonight we have a common enemy.

The trespassers.

If it weren't for them, everything would be just fine like it always is. Dad wouldn't be forcing me to leave and there wouldn't be all this strangeness between me, Ronan, and Raegan.

But it's not fine.

The trespassers showed up, stirred our happy pot, and are ruining our lives. My parents may not see it yet, but it's as clear as day to me.

If I have to go, they do too.

"Where are they staying?" Wild asks, creeping to a stop before we make it to the glow of the fire. "In the big house?"

"There," I whisper, pointing to a couple of tents in the far corner, hidden in the dark shadows of the night.

Wild leads the way, slipping from tree to tree to remain hidden from the few remaining people who are walking around or sitting by the fire. Chet follows behind him, crunching loudly, and I follow up the rear in near silence. We manage to make our way over to the tents without being seen by anyone.

When Dad finds out we kicked their asses, he'll be furious. But it's not like he can do anything worse than he's already done. Being banished from my family is the absolute worst. If anything, I have an inkling of hope that maybe he'll decide Wild is a bad influence and want to keep me from going back with him.

It's a huge hope, but one I'm going to lean into anyway.

The three of us huddle just outside the tents to come up with a game plan. It's decided that Wild will grab Jace and Chet will grab CJ. Then I'll punch the fuckers until I can't punch anymore. Sounds like a solid plan to me. My blood practically buzzes with anticipation as it rushes through my veins. I crack my neck and then pop each one of my knuckles to ready myself. Just before we make our move, I hear it.

A giggle.

A *familiar* giggle.

Why is Raegan in the tent with that fucker?

The betrayal hits like a well-placed kick to the balls. It stuns me, fucking hurts, and then just pisses me off. How could she want to be near him after what they said about Destiny?

Wild arches a brow at me, clearly figuring out who the laughter belongs to. He's waiting for me to call it. Do we continue with the plan or do we turn back?

Raegan laughs again.

And then again.

What's so great about CJ that she keeps fucking around with him?

Is she doing it to piss me off?

My thoughts are a hurricane of confusion and rage. Behind the haze of fury that's heightened by alcohol, I remember that she doesn't know about what CJ and Jace said about Destiny.

In that case, I have to protect her.

Protect her from what she doesn't know.

As her older brother, it's my duty.

Tossing out the plan, I charge past Wild and Chet. As I approach, I can see the silhouettes of four people huddled in the tent together. If I had a knife on me, I'd shred the material to get to Raegan. Instead, I have to settle for grabbing the zipper and yanking it up with enough force, the entire tent shudders.

"Ryder!" Raegan hisses upon seeing my unmasked fury. "What the hell?! You scared the crap out of me!"

Ignoring the pandemonium within the tent, I keep my focus on one thing. Her. Raegan. My sister. She lets out a surprised shriek when I grab hold of her arm and drag her out of the tent. Since she's tiny, she's no match for my brute strength. I haul her out of the tent despite her hissing and scratching like a bobcat. Wild roars with laughter until he sees Sadie pop her head out of the tent. Then, he and Chet snag her with the same urgency.

None of our girls are safe with those fuckers.

I squat and then hoist Raegan up, easily tossing her over one shoulder. She's a mean bitch sometimes and won't go down without a fight. I grunt each time her fists slam into my kidneys. That shit is going to leave bruises.

Saving her from CJ and Jace is worth a million bruises.

"You're an asshole, Ryder Jamison!" she bellows. "I'm telling Dad!"

Fuck if I care.

Doesn't matter.

I'm gone soon anyway.

I smack her hard on her jean-clad ass, which causes her to howl in fury. She manages to lift my shirt up and digs her fingernails into my lower back. Based on the severe burn left in their wake, I'd say she most certainly broke the skin.

Again, still worth it.

"Calm the fuck down," I growl, swatting her ass again, this time much harder like Dad does when someone's done something especially bad. "Keep it up and I'll take a belt to your ass!"

"You are not my father, you piece of shit!"

We carry on like this all the way across the yard. I'm pretty sure if Dad isn't still awake, he will be now. Not that I care anymore.

I manage to get her back to my cabin. Ronan opens the cabin door, confusion marring his face when he sees that I have our sister captive. He steps out of the way and I charge over to my bed. I toss her onto the mattress and glower down at her.

"Not fucking cool, Rae," I snarl, fury bubbling up inside of me and spilling over. "You may as well have fucked the enemy."

"Ryder," Ronan starts, grabbing onto my shoulder. "What the hell happened?"

Raegan sits up on her knees, face red and eyes glowing with rage. "He can't stand the fact I have friends!"

"Friends?" I spit out. "More like fuck buddies."

She lunges at me, but I shove her easily back onto the bed. Ronan shoots me a disproving look before standing between us.

"You were with CJ and Jace?" Ronan asks, voice lowering. "Why?"

Raegan sneers at us. "Oh, so you're choosing his side? I thought we were best friends! Just because you two…" She bites down hard on her bottom lip, trapping the words in her mouth.

Wild, Chet, and Sadie's footsteps can be heard

behind us as they enter the cabin, making it quickly too crowded.

"Don't stop on our account," Wild taunts. "What were you two doing?"

Ronan's neck flashes crimson and his shoulders tighten. Raegan scowls, not making contact with anyone.

Did he tell her?

Seriously?

"You're not allowed to see them," I growl, ignoring Wild altogether. "The trespassers are bad, Rae. They're fucking warped."

She scoffs, eyes snaring mine again. "Are you jealous?"

Wild snorts and Chet cracks up laughing. Fucking pricks.

"No." I pin her with a harsh glare. "They were talking shit."

"So? You idiots talk shit all the time," she tosses back, waving a hand back and forth between me and Wild. "What makes them any worse?"

"Rae," Ronan says quietly, taking her hand. "Jace was talking shit about Dez."

Her brows furl together and she darts a glance my way. "What did they say?"

Wild throws his big-ass body onto the bed beside her and sits up on one elbow, grinning evilly. "Jace wants to fuck her. Thinks she's hot."

Sadie squawks out in surprise. "Wait. She's like fourteen. Those guys are in their twenties. Yuck."

"Now you tell me?" Raegan says, deflating like a balloon. "I didn't know."

Ronan squeezes onto the bed between her and Wild, who watches them both with interest. I love Wild like a cousin, but tonight he's in the way. He's costing me precious time with my two favorite people in my family. I wish I could make him and his friends leave already.

"If I didn't know any better," Wild says with a dark chuckle, "I'd say the three of you are fucking."

All of us whip our heads in his direction. Ronan's neck flashes bright red and Raegan gapes at him. I just want to push my siblings out of the way so I can throttle him.

"Shut up, Wild," I bite out. "You know we're not doing that shit. That'd be incest and that can't fucking happen." I scrub a palm over my face. "Not that I'd even want it to."

Lies.

My emotions are a goddamn mess right now, forever tangled up with my sister and brother.

Wild sits back up and drapes an arm over Ronan's shoulder before smirking my way. "I thought it ran in the family."

Everyone is quiet, waiting for him to elaborate. He howls with laughter until tears are rolling down his face. My hands curl into fists and I'm seconds from beating the words out of him.

"What are you even talking about?" I demand. "You're talking shit just like those idiots out there."

Wild's humor fades and he gives a sharp shake of his head. "You really don't know?"

"Don't know what?" Raegan hisses. "That you're an asshole? We're all plenty aware, Wild Knox."

"Takes one to know one, wifey." He ignores her huff of indignation and grins at me. "Dude. Your dad is your mom's dad."

Chet mutters a curse word under his breath and Sadie makes a choked sound. Meanwhile, me and my two siblings are silent.

"You done making shit up to scandalize your friends?" I snarl, glowering at him.

"Your taunts and lies are boring," Raegan snaps at him. "Right, Ronan?"

Ronan has turned to look at Wild, a frown on his face. "What are you saying?"

"Man, I'm not fucking with you. I overheard our dads reminiscing on our last visit, when they were shit-faced drunk, about how they didn't like each other in the beginning." Wild's gaze bounces from Ronan to Raegan and then settles on me. "My dad brought your mom books about incest and shit. Devon is Reed's daughter."

Devon is Reed's daughter.

My mother is my father's daughter.

What the actual fuck?

CHAPTER TWENTY-THREE

raegan

H E'S INSANE.

And a liar.

Mom and Dad are husband and wife, not daughter and father. That's just gross.

"I hate you," I hiss at Wild. "You just never know when to stop. Always making stuff up to get a rise out of us, especially me. Well, dumbass, we're not falling for it."

Wild rolls his eyes at me. "Fucking with you is fun, but I'm serious. Go ask your dad right now. Or is he your grandpa? Your family tree is a shitshow."

I lunge for him, ready to give him a matching black eye, but Ronan physically holds me back. He's never rough with me, but his hold bites into my flesh, bruising me.

"Let go of me." I jerk from his hold and nearly fall off the bed in my escape. Ryder, forgetting about our fight, snags my arm to save me from the fall. "Let. Go. Of. Me."

Ryder's nostrils flare as he glares down at me but then releases me without a word. I shove past him and take Sadie's hand.

"Go straight to Ronan's cabin," Ryder calls after me, voice deep and authoritative like Dad's.

I drag Sadie out of the cabin with me, taking great pleasure in slamming the door behind me. I'm about to haul her next door when a giggle makes me freeze.

Mya.

I let go of Sadie and whirl around to the sound. Mya is sprawled out on Ryder's hammock, smiling sweetly at me. The guys continue to talk, their voices carrying beyond the closed door.

How much did she hear?

"Aww, poor girl," Mya says in a mocking tone. "Her family's dark, dirty secrets are coming out."

Sadie, even though she's friends with dumbass Wild, is actually cool. She comes to stand beside me, arms crossing over her chest, in a show of solidarity. Emboldened by having a partner against this bitch, I narrow my eyes and sneer at Mya.

"Go back to whatever hole you crawled out of." I wriggle my fingers at her. "You're a family full of snakes and we don't want your kind here."

Mya sits up in the hammock and cocks her head to the side as she studies me. I don't back down, holding my ground with a hateful expression on my face that does wonders to make my baby brothers wither any-time I flash it their way.

Unbothered, her reptilian-looking lips curl into a sinister grin. I'm surprised she doesn't grow venomous fangs and try to bite me. "It's true, you know. It's why our family is always looking for fresh blood. Well, fresh bloodline anyway."

My blood runs icy cold in my veins. I don't like the fact she overheard what we were all discussing and is now trying to punish me with it.

"Wild's a liar," Sadie offers weakly. "He just likes getting people riled up. You'll be smart to learn that now."

Mya completely ignores Sadie as though she's an unimportant gnat buzzing around her prey. I'm not some little mouse she can swallow, though. I will tear Mya to pieces with my fingernails, my words, and my knife if I have to.

"It explains the birth defects," Mya continues, her smile widening.

"There's nothing wrong with me," I snarl, lip curling up in disgust. "Nice try."

Mya scoffs, shaking her head. "Oh, there's plenty wrong with you, starting with your face, but I wasn't talking about you. I was talking about your little sister."

The cabin door creaks open and Ryder crowds in behind me, his body heat and smell enveloping me like a warm hug. I'm so pissed at him, but I'm thankful he's here to help me deal with this lying witch.

"What about Destiny?" Ryder demands.

Mya climbs out of the hammock and shoots Ryder a saucy grin that boils my blood. "Oh, hey, Ryder."

"Mya." Ryder's hand settles on my shoulder. "Spit it out."

She eyes the way his fingers curl around me, keeping me in his possessive hold. Or maybe he's trying to hold me back from clawing her eyeballs out. Either way, I like the way it feels, even if I am still mad. That no matter what, we're still on the same side. Family sticks together.

"Destiny is blind because what Wild said was true. She has a birth defect. It's obvious as to how that came to be. Why do you think you people have lived out here in the wilderness for so long away from civilization?" Mya lifts a brow and motions at the forest beyond our fence. "Have you not noticed your parents' significant age gap?"

Ryder's grip tightens nearly to the point of pain, but I let the sensation ground me. If not for his hold, I'd have lost myself to blind fury and given her a black eye that looks like Wild's. It still might be in her future.

I will not rise to her bait.

But she's right, *right*?

Dad *is* much older than Mom.

Still, despite their obvious age gap, Mya is wrong. What she's saying is ridiculous and impossible.

"Oh, come on," she says with a cackle of laughter. "Devon could be your sister." Another giggle, this one cruel. "Wait. That's right. She technically is."

Another person sidles up beside me and slips their hand into mine. Ronan. With my brothers at my side and at my back, I can almost ignore this vicious viper. Almost.

"When you go to sleep, I will find you in your bed," I whisper, baring my teeth at her. "And I'll cut your hair off. Maybe I'll blind *you* while I'm at it!"

Mya laughs as she sashays off the porch and disappears into the darkness.

Sadie sighs heavily and says, "What a psychopath. I'm going to bed."

The three of us remain frozen long after the cabin door closes next door. I can hear Wild and Chet murmuring from inside Ryder's cabin. Finally, the three of us are alone after the bombs that've been dropped.

"It makes sense now why Dad is making me…" Ryder trails off, not bothering to finish his sentence. He snatches his hand back as though my shoulder is drenched in poison. "Fuck."

Ronan's hand is cold in mine. Stiff and unmoving. His head is bowed, eyes squeezed shut. He releases my hand and shifts slightly away from me.

"It's all lies, obviously," I say shakily, hating the sudden loneliness hollowing out my chest. "We can't believe what they say."

Emotion clogs my throat when neither of my brothers agrees with me.

Ryder begins pacing the porch, fingers tugging at his dark hair. He's growing it out at the moment, so it's thick enough to grab onto. I like it best when he buzzes it. The prickly hair feels good on my fingertips.

I give my head a quick shake to clear away those thoughts. Thinking about my hands on my brother's head after what Wild and Mya said sends a shiver down my spine. Hugging my arms to me, desperately needing warmth on my chilled body, I look away from him, this time at Ronan.

Ronan slowly makes it over to the steps and sits down. His shoulders hunch forward as he hugs his knees to his chest. The air is thick with tension—each of us mentally battling the accusation Wild claimed and Mya agreed with.

It's not true.

They're both terrible liars who get off on tormenting us, especially me.

I certainly don't believe them.

My brothers, however, have taken the news hard. Ryder stalks back and forth with the agitation of a crazed mountain lion—half starved, half mad from disease. His shoulders are taut and the muscles in his neck keep flexing as though he's clenching his teeth. Ronan, on the other hand, is a granite statue of despair. He doesn't move or make a sound.

"We can't believe their lies," I say softly, hoping just the two of them will hear. I'm not about to let Wild or Mya, who might be lurking nearby, listen to our private conversation.

Neither brother says anything. Anger prickles through me, lighting up every nerve ending. I'm annoyed that these two are allowing Wild to screw with their heads. When Ryder stalks past me again on his never-ending pacing quest, I seize his bicep with my hand.

His blue eyes are dark and intense as they bore into me. The heat of his stare ignites a small fire deep in my core. Warmth settles there and also ripples its way through my body. My face grows hot under his fiery scrutiny.

"Don't be naive, Rae."

After spitting out those harsh words, he tugs his arm from my hold and then walks over to where Ronan is sitting. He takes a seat beside him close enough the sides of their bodies touch.

Jealousy snares me in its trap and I practically hiss with fury. The reminder of what Ronan told me they did together explodes inside me. I want to shove them apart and sit right between them. Ronan's body leans toward Ryder's, closing the gap completely. He slumps against our brother as though he has the power to make everything better. To my absolute horror, Ryder relaxes and then wraps an arm around Ronan.

No.

Tears burn at my eyes and I have to blink furiously to keep them at bay. I want to yell at them and call them awful names, but I know that'll push them even closer together, squeezing me out completely. With a ragged sigh, drowning with emotion, I walk over to the steps and sit down on Ryder's other side. Mirroring Ronan, I lean against Ryder.

If he rejects me now, after everything, I'll—

My mind calms when Ryder shifts to put an arm around me also. It does wonders to soothe my scattered, heartbroken thoughts. I edge closer to Ryder, inhaling his masculine scent with a hint of liquor. His large palm settles on my hip and he strokes his thumb over me so tenderly I almost cry. Again.

"Destiny is perfect," I murmur, voice strained and sad. "She is."

This time, my brothers speak. In unison. "She is."

I let out a ragged sigh of relief. A hot tear rolls down my cheek and clings to my jaw. Swallowing hard, I hold back a sniffle so they don't hear my despair.

And that's what this is.

Despair.

Confusion.

Betrayal.

I may not believe Wild or Mya, but the seed of doubt has been planted. It's festering and growing, starting with my two brothers. Because I care deeply about them and are attuned to their feelings, I'm not immune. It's getting to me too.

Ronan takes my hand again. It's still cold as he threads his fingers with mine and settles it on Ryder's warm thigh. Ryder's palm slides up my back and then he's gently stroking my hair. I'm confused by the gesture until I realize I'm sniffling despite my efforts not to.

He's comforting me.

This has my chest tightening and more tears

forming. It takes a monumental effort to keep the sob lodged in my throat. Ronan makes a sound that's pained. We're hurting. We're all three hurting, once again, from these outsiders.

Ryder's hand strokes through my hair and then he palms my back, rubbing me in large circles. He's never been one to comfort us. That's always been Ronan. Seeing this side of Ryder softens hard places deep inside my heart. I wish everyone were gone so the three of us could cuddle in Ryder's bed and sleep just like this, snuggled against one another.

As Ryder's fingers curl around my ribs under my arms, I suck in a sharp breath. His touch feels intimate now. Forbidden. I bite my lip in anticipation, letting my thoughts run wild. Achingly slow, he inches his hand upward, closer to my armpit. When his fingertips brush against the side of my breast, a whining sound rattles from my throat.

Ryder is touching my breast.

Not the whole thing. Just a gentle graze of his fingers. But still a purposeful touch.

I'm about to twist my body to give him further access when footsteps thud through the cabin and then the door opens. The fear of facing more ridicule from Wild has me jolting out of both Ronan's and Ryder's holds, making me stagger down the steps and onto the grass.

I don't say a word to any of them, choosing to dart next door as quickly as possible. I sneak into the cabin and find Sadie already fast asleep on a sleeping bag on the floor. Destiny's soft breathing can be heard from the bed. Mage is curled up next to her, his little wolf head poking out from under the covers. I quickly change out of my clothes and into my pajamas before sliding into bed next to my sister.

How dare anyone suggest there's something wrong with her?

There's not.

And screw Jace and CJ for talking shit about my sister. Whatever friendship I thought I had with them is over. I'm Team Ryder. The trespassers need to go. Wild can go right along with them for all I care.

I hug her close to me and inhale her sweet scent. I'll protect her from the words of others. I'll protect her from everyone.

CHAPTER TWENTY-FOUR

ronan

EVERYTHING IS ALL FUCKED-UP.

Yes, I'm annoyed at Wild for stating his bull-shit lies, but I'm more bothered by how Ryder's been acting. He hasn't smiled or laughed since he spoke to Dad the night after our…tent rendezvous. Things only worsened when he caught Raegan hanging out with the enemy. Wild and Mya didn't help when they stirred up their shit.

I just want everything to go back to normal.

I want them to leave. All of them.

I just want it to be me, Raegan, and Ryder again. Sneaking out to swim in the creek, hunting, fishing, reading, hanging out. Just us.

Ryder's been missing since early this morning when Rowdy came for him. My guess is they went hunting. Since I need a minute to myself and my thoughts, I choose to help the littles and Mom gather eggs in the chicken coup.

The morning sun hits Mom's golden hair and makes it shimmer. Her smile is wide as she squats down beside Kota and Declan with Dawson sleeping in the baby carrier on her back. She's really beautiful. And young. So young compared to our father.

Anxiety sours my gut. What if what Wild claimed is true? What if Mom really is Dad's daughter? Bile creeps up my throat. We'd all be at risk for birth defects. Maybe that's why I'm attracted to men when I'm supposed to want a woman.

If I were Raegan or even Ryder, I'd have the balls to come out and ask Mom. Right now when she's caught off guard and doesn't have a chance to make anything up. I could discover the truth with one bold question.

And yet, I bite my tongue.

Knowledge isn't always power. Knowledge can be pain. It can maim and destroy. In the case of this accusation that she'd marry her own father and have children with him, I realize I don't want to know. I'm okay with being blissfully ignorant.

"Everything okay, Ro?" Mom asks, her lips tugging into a concerned frown. "You're looking a little sad lately. I'm worried about you."

My heart squeezes in my chest. I am a little sad lately, but I can't tell her. I refuse to. This family already feels as though it's brittle and my problems might be what completely shatters us. Not happening. Ever.

"All good, Mom," I lie, grinning brightly at her.

She scrutinizes me, eyes skimming all over my face

as though she can see right inside my head. I keep the too-wide grin stretched over my face, though it begins to shake slightly. I think I might have her fooled…

"Ronan, baby," she begins with a sigh. "Depression runs in our family." Her features shutter at a past memory that momentarily holds her hostage. "Promise me you'll talk to me before you let whatever's bothering you completely consume you."

"Promise." My forced smile falters, so I look away before she can see it. "I'll run these up to the big house."

She purses her lips together, studying me for a beat, and then nods, handing me the basket she and the little ones have been filling with eggs. I grab my own basket and hurry out of the coup before she's able to dig any deeper. In my haste, I nearly railroad over my brother.

Ryder side-steps me and raises his arm holding his rifle, eyes wide as he assesses me.

"Sorry," I grumble. "I just had to get out of there."

His gaze travels past me to where Mom can be seen in the coup. I watch as his features harden into stone. The last thing I need right now is Ryder confronting Mom about what Wild said.

"Here," I say, thrusting one of the baskets at him. "I think we need to talk."

Ryder shoulders his rifle before taking the basket. The angry, determined expression on his face has faded into something more resigned. I don't like either of those looks. I want my happy, smiling brother back.

Together, we walk in silence past the visitors sitting

at the firepit. I notice Logan watching me with narrowed eyes. It's nearly impossible not to squirm, but I somehow manage, focusing on Ryder's and my feet as we step in perfect unison. Thankfully, when we make it into the big house, no one is lingering in the kitchen.

We're alone.

"How'd the hunt go?" I ask, opting for small talk instead of going right into what I really want to ask him. *What happened with Dad?*

"Rowdy almost got a buck. We're going to leave some corn tonight and go back earlier tomorrow to see if we can stake him out." Ryder follows me into the large pantry and leans against the doorframe as I start putting the eggs in the crate. "You can come with us if you want."

I finish unloading my basket and then take his before answering. "Yeah, maybe."

He sighs heavily. "What do you want to talk about?"

I set the basket down at my feet and turn to look at him. Today, he's tired. I can see it in the slight shadowing under his eyes, the hunch of his shoulders, and the inability to even attempt a smile. Even his voice sounds exhausted.

"What's going on with you?" I step closer to him. "You've been distant."

His Adam's apple bobs as he swallows, darting his eyes away from mine. "It's nothing."

"Big liar."

I poke at his stomach that's hard from a life of

physical labor. He jerks his head my way, a smirk playing at his lips. Seeing the tease of a smile I've been missing has my stomach flipping. Memories of that night flood through my brain, sending currents of electricity pulsing through me straight to my cock. I'm annoyed by the fact I'm sporting a semi just from an almost smile from my brother, but here I am doing just that.

"Tell me," I murmur. "You can tell me anything. We don't keep secrets, Ry."

His blue eyes flash at the mention of secrets and his tongue runs along his bottom lip, wetting it. My own mouth waters for a taste of his bottom lip. I'd love to nip at it and turn it into his full-on boyish grin.

As though he's trapped in a trance, he reaches forward, hooking his finger through the front belt hoop of my jeans. I choke on a gasp as he tugs me closer to him. My heart leaps up my throat and every nerve in my body sings to life.

Yes. Yes. Yes.

His touch and attention, even as simple as this stolen moment in the pantry, are a fantasy come to life. It's wrong, but right now, I don't care. This feels really good—us, alone, focused on one another.

I want to kiss him.

Again.

This time with tongues and teeth and breathy moans.

I blink away my daze and understanding chases away the lust I'd been consumed by. He's trying to distract me. He's playing my desire for him against me to avoid the question. Hurt lances through me, cutting deeply and violently. I jerkily pull away from him, swatting his hand off my belt hoop. My cheeks are hot with a mixture of lingering desire and embarrassment.

I fell for it.

He laid a trap, much like he plans to for that buck, and he pounced.

"Ro," Ryder says, panic flickering in his eyes. "I…I can't."

I cross my arms over my chest and glower at him. "You can. Tell me and stop playing games to confuse me." My voice quivers. "That's fucked-up to lead me on like that."

His eyebrows pinch together and he squeezes his eyes shut. A heavy sigh rushes past his lips—lips I was craving desperately seconds ago. A liar's lips. "I wasn't leading you on."

Now his liar's lips are spilling audible lies.

"Look at you," I hiss. "You don't even care. You were just doing what you knew would distract me to avoid a stupid question."

Oh God.

This is so messed up and it's all my fault. I let him get me off the other night and press a kiss to my lips. I basically begged for it. But he's never wanted any of this. It's all been out of some duty to help me, his brother, and today, avoid my line of questioning.

Unbelievable.

"I care," Ryder says, unable to look at me as despair consumes him. "I care so much it fucking kills me."

All the indignant fire burning through me swooshes out to make way for guilt. Guilt may as well be my middle name.

"Then why won't you tell me?" I demand, my voice a mere whisper. "Please."

His jaw tightens as he sears me with his gaze. "Dad's making me leave."

"Leave to go where?" I frown as I try to make sense of his words. "What does that even mean?"

He sets down his rifle, propping it up against the shelves, and then cautiously approaches me. This time, he's not looking at me like he wants to kiss me. His eyes are searching mine, pleading with me to understand. He raises his hand like he wants to cradle my face in his palm. I'm desperate enough for his touch, I almost tilt my head to meet him halfway.

Almost.

When he realizes I'm not going to let him get away with this twice, he gives up, dropping his hand to his side. His nostrils flare in frustration. "It means when Wild and them go back to town, I'm going with them."

My heart stutters to a stop as I gape at him. "What? For how long? Why?"

"As long as it takes to find a wife," he mutters, scowling. "Indefinitely if need be."

I'm already shaking my head. "N-No. You can't leave us. You can't leave us!"

He swallows and shrugs. "It's out of my hands."

"Why would he do this to us?" I demand, rubbing at the center of my chest. An ache has formed there and I want it to go away. It grows wider and wider by the second. I realize that hole is where Ryder lives and he's being excavated by my dad's stupid order. "Why, Ryder? Why?"

His mouth parts as he prepares to speak, but a blood-curdling scream pierces the air. Since Ryder is closer to the pantry door, he turns on his heel and is out before me. I follow him toward the sounds of continued screaming toward the makeshift infirmary that used to be Dez and Raegan's room.

Stacey must be in labor.

Ryder slams to a halt just inside the doorway, forcing me to step around him so I can see. Stacey is crying and screaming, but she's not the one in pain here.

It's Kristen.

Kristen, face chalky and eyes wild, slashes another red stripe across the flesh of her forearm near her wrist. Blood slides down her arm, puddling on the white sheet that's tangled in her lap. She's about to slash a third time before I snap into action.

"No!" I bellow, rushing her. "Stop!"

She grunts when I grab onto the wrist of her uninjured arm. I squeeze tight enough she lets the steak knife drop. It slides to the floor with a clatter.

"Fuck," I cry out. "Ryder, get Dad!"

Kristen sobs, her entire body trembling. I snatch up

the sheet and apply it to her bleeding arm, hoping to staunch the flow. I glance over at Stacey, but she's gone, having followed Ryder out of the room. Carter is here with us, but he's sleeping off his intense pain and unmoving, therefore no help to us right now.

"Everything's going to be okay," I promise to Kristen. "I've got you."

It's a promise I can't keep, though. We're hours away from civilization. If she bleeds out or gets an infection, she'll die. There's no access to medical care.

Kristen turns her pale, tearstained face toward me and pins me with a frantic look. "Run."

Run?

Great, she's already speaking incoherently. She's probably seconds away from death.

"We're going to get you fixed up," I say, ignoring her strange command. "My parents have sewn up their fair share of gashes. You're going to be good as new very soon."

Kristen grabs the front of my shirt and twists the material in her fist. The panic in her eyes chills me to my very soul. "You have to run! Save yourself!"

What the hell does that mean?

Is she that messed up by what those men did to her that she's behaving irrationally?

Heavy footsteps thud into the room. Logan leads the group, followed by Dad and Ryder. I'm steered away from Kristen as Dad sets to inspect her self-inflicted wounds while Logan hugs her tight, kissing her head.

"I've got you, babe. You're safe now. No one can hurt you. Not even you." Logan rains kisses down on her head and face like she's the most precious thing in the world to him. "I've got you. Forever, remember? I promised you forever."

Days ago, I might've been jealous at his sweet words.

Today, I'm battling my own demons.

I glance over at Ryder, who wears a pensive expression. He's my brother. That's supposed to mean forever and yet he's leaving without argument.

He can't leave.

I won't let him.

I've got you, Ryder. Forever. I'm promising you forever.

CHAPTER TWENTY-FIVE

raegan

I'M HOLLOW INSIDE.

After last night, my emotions are thin, barely hanging on by a thread. I was thankful no one could see me crying myself to sleep.

In the past, whenever I was sad or frustrated, Ronan was always there. It was him in the bed with me, listening to me rant and rave while offering me much-needed comfort. His shoulder I leaned on. The sound of his laugh that made me cheer up.

I miss him.

I miss the easy times we had together.

Before all this. Before the confusing shift with Ryder and the turmoil of the trespassers. Before Wild showed up with his stupid lies.

I'm leaned up against the side of the big house behind a tree under Kota and Declan's window, hiding from having to do any chores, when Mage and Spirit dart past me, yipping at each other. Those pups double in size each day, I swear.

I'm still staring after the wolf pups when I notice Ronan has come to stand at the edge of the house. He's scrubbing at his hands with a cloth frantically. Concern has me hopping to my feet, abandoning my hideout, to check on him.

Blood.

His hands are covered in it.

"Ro, what happened?" I demand as I rush over to him. "Are you hurt?"

Upon seeing me, he visibly relaxes, which does wonders to take my own edge off. "It's not mine. It's Kristen's."

I take the damp cloth from him and start to clean his hands for him since he was absently scrubbing in the same spot over and over. "Is she okay?"

His pained eyes pin me. "She…She tried to kill herself."

"What?" I gape at him in shock. "Why?"

"Those rapists really fucked her up, Rae. She was speaking all sorts of nonsense. They made her crazy!"

I tear my gaze from his to focus on cleaning him off. He'll have to take a dip in the river to scrub the blood from beneath his nails, but at least I've gotten most of it off.

"Is she okay?" I ask, taking his hand in mine. "Are *you* okay?"

"Dad's sewing her up. He said they're flesh

wounds and look worse than they are." Ronan sighs and drops a head on my shoulder. "I, uh, I had to hold pressure to her cuts. I was terrified of messing up. Logan would've hated me for letting his wife die."

My hackles rise at the mention of one of them. Ronan shouldn't give a damn about what those people think about him. But he's always been the most tenderhearted of the three of us. I wouldn't have him any other way.

"You're awfully sad about this woman we barely know," I murmur, giving his hand a squeeze. "Are you letting Wild's lies get to you?"

He lifts his head off my shoulder and looks down at his feet. "Nah, it's not that."

"Well, if it is, I understand. It bothers me too, which is why I'm going to confront Mom and Dad today."

Ronan snaps his attention to me and frowns. "W-What? Why?"

"Because I need to hear it from them that it's not true. That they didn't willingly put all their kids' lives in danger. I have to know."

He shakes his head, eyes flaring with panic. "You can't."

"Why not?" I scoff at him.

His hand pulls out of mine and he runs his bloodstained fingers through his messy hair. "Because they'll send you away too, Raegan. I can't lose you too!"

Every muscle in my body stiffens as I let his words sink in. They're cold and ominous. A threat of something that's going to destroy me. I know this because the heartbreak that's making his eyes glassy and his bottom lip shaky will destroy me too.

"Who's being sent away?" I choke out. "Who, Ro?"

Somehow, I know.

I can feel it in my bones.

But I need to hear it.

"Rowdy?" I ask, voice squeaky. "It fucked him up last time. He's broken now."

"Forget I said anything," Ronan mutters, tearing his eyes from mine to focus on something unimportant behind me. "It's nothing."

Great. So now my own brother and best friend is going to lie to me too. Everyone in this freaking state is a liar and I'm so over it. It certainly makes me want to hitch a ride with stupid Wild out of here so I can start a life away from all the liars.

Now who's the liar, liar?

"It's not nothing. Tell me, dammit!" I shriek, shoving at his shoulder. "So help me, Ronan, if you don't tell me, I'll—"

"They're sending Ryder away." His teeth grind together and his jaw muscle flexes. "They're sending him away because they're worried he'll get you pregnant."

What?

Is he joking right now?

Based on the horrified expression on his face, I realize he's not.

My parents are clearly insane.

I stagger away from my brother shaking my head. "That's stupid. He's not going to get me pregnant. I don't even want any stupid babies!"

Ronan says nothing and won't meet my eyes.

"They're hypocrites," I snarl. "If what Wild says is true, then they're lying hypocrites. How dare them!"

As Ronan's words sink in, my heart feels as though it's shattering into a million tiny pieces, turning into sand and being washed away by the river of deceit. Yes, *deceit.*

"Ryder told you, but he didn't tell me?" I ask, voice shaking with a mixture of anger and devastation. "It's always been you two with me as an afterthought."

Ronan huffs in frustration. "No, Rae, he literally just told me!"

"He should have told us together!" Tears of hurt prickle at my eyes, but I refuse to let Ronan see them. I turn my head upward toward the overcast skies and let out a bellow of rage. "You two always have your secrets and you make each other come!"

Ronan makes a garbled choking sound. "You promised you'd keep that quiet. Rae, calm down. This is why no one ever tells you anything!"

His words strike me and I stumble backward.

Anger flickers in his eyes, but he's also ashamed and afraid. Ronan reminds me of a cornered animal, shaking and baring his teeth like he might bite.

"Ronan?" a deep voice calls out. "Can you help me, man?"

Ronan pins me with a hard stare before turning on his heel, not saying another word to me. I helplessly watch as he makes his way over to Logan. Logan mentions something about Ronan helping him get Kristen back to his tent where he can keep a better eye on her.

And just like that, I've been abandoned.

My heart aches something terrible. I want to drop to the ground, curl into a fetal position, and cry. Ronan snapped at me and Ryder's leaving. Oh, and my parents might be related to each other. A tidal wave of crushing sadness threatens to drown me. For a moment, I almost let it.

But then anger prowls in like a rabid predator, salivating and hungry to sink its teeth into something or someone. I tap into that emotion, letting all the sad, helpless victimized feelings erode completely.

I want blood.

There's only one person who can handle it.

Coincidentally, he's also the person I'm most angry with.

Ryder.

I take off running on a mad search for my older brother. He's not in the big house that's crawling with concerned people. He's not in his cabin or Ronan's. He's not in the chicken coup or in the goat pen. He's not by the fire where Wild, Sadie, and Chet are laughing.

He's gone.

Not permanently, though. At least not yet.

I slip out the gate past one of the men who does a shitty job staying on watch and take off to the stairs that lead to the river. If he's not here, he'll be at Rowdy's cabin. I'm almost at the stairs when I see him leaned against a tree, scowling at the earth at his booted feet.

Resignation paints his normally admittedly hand-some features and I hate it. I want to punch the look off his face and replace it with the fierce, determined expression he gets when we fight. So I charge at him, not giving him a second to react.

"Oof!"

We both go down into the brush as I tackle him at a full speed run. He doesn't have a chance to even know what hit him. I wrench my knife from the sheath and dig it into the soft, fleshy part of his skin under his chin.

"You're leaving," I cry out. "You're leaving and you never planned to tell me!"

His eyes narrow and flash. I love seeing the pissed off look he gives me a lot of the times. It's much bet-ter than the sad, woe is me one he's been sporting lately. "I didn't have a chance."

"Liar!" I smack his cheek with my free hand while keeping a firm grip on the hilt of the knife. "You could have told us together!"

He grabs hold of my smacking hand, gripping so tight I know I'll never get away unless I hack through his wrist with my knife. "I'm sorry."

"That's it? You're sorry? Aren't you even going to try to fight them on this?"

"What can I do, Rae?" Ryder snarls. "Dad's word is law."

"Yeah, and he's a hypocrite!"

"It's done," he mutters. "I'm sorry, but the decision has been made."

I struggle to free my hand to no avail and opt for pressing the tip of the blade harder into his flesh. He grunts in pain and then a droplet of blood races down his neck.

"It's stupid," I choke out. "You're not going to get me pregnant! You don't even like me. You're too busy making Ronan come!" A sob catches in my throat and I hate its very presence. "You two have shut me out."

With lightning speed and complete surprise to me, Ryder flips us. It happens so fast, I don't realize it's happened until I'm staring up at him, his heavy, muscular body pinning mine. He grabs hold of the knife and tosses it several feet away.

"I don't like you?" Ryder hisses, disgust lacing his words. "Are you fucking kidding me right now?"

I glower up at him because it's better than crying. "I said what I said."

He shifts his body until his lower body is pressing against my pussy through our clothes. During our struggle, he's managed to wedge himself between my thighs. The sudden realization of our position has heat flooding through me and making my core pulse with need.

"I…" Ryder looks away and swallows before turning his fiery gaze back on me. "I more than like you, Rae. I fucking love you. And not in some stupid sibling way either. It's why I have to leave."

I blink at him in shock. "What?"

"I said what I said," he says with a smirk, mirroring my own words back at me. "But it doesn't matter. We can't do this shit. It's not right. Bad things can happen to our babies."

Our babies.

For someone who never wanted kids, I sure as hell love the sound of those words.

"Blindness is not a birth defect, dumbass. Lots of people are blind and that's not because they had sex with their sister. It's just a thing that happens to some people. Like being deaf. I've read lots about disabilities." I'm not sure if I'm totally right, but I'd say just about anything to convince him otherwise. "It's just biology and maybe God too."

"Regardless, nothing can happen. Dad won't allow it."

Anger swells up inside me again and I open my mouth to tell him where Dad can shove it, but then he's swiftly moving toward me. Ryder's surprisingly soft lips press to mine. They're gentle at first and then he parts them. My own lips follow his motions. I groan when his tongue slips into my mouth, seeking out my own.

Oh my God.

Ryder is kissing me.

And it's nothing like the slick, playful motions CJ offered with his. Knowing now that there's a difference, I can't believe I even kissed CJ in the first place.

This kiss is *everything*.

It consumes every cell in my body and wakes up parts of me I never knew existed.

Every thought inside my head turns dark so that all I hear, see, feel is him. Ryder's possessive, exploring tongue. Ryder's muffled moans of pleasure. Ryder's dark eyelashes fanned over his cheeks.

I find myself digging my heels into his ass, drawing him closer. He's hard everywhere, especially his cock. It presses against my sweet spot, sending desire lashing at every nerve ending in my body.

I want my clothes off so I can feel his skin on mine.

I want to cling to him like this in the river as it rushes around us. To feel him inside me as we kiss like there's no tomorrow.

"Fuck, I'll miss you," he murmurs over my lips

before biting on the bottom lip. "You taste so god-damn perfect like I dreamed of."

His words flutter over me like petals from a flower, soft and delicate, teasing my skin into goose bumps.

This is wrong, right?

So why does it feel so good?

His palm slides under my T-shirt and I gasp at the feel of his rough, calloused fingertips on my ribs. I squirm beneath him, lashing my own tongue against his, needing him to take whatever he can get from me. He must understand my need because his thumb grazes the underside of my breast over my bra.

I want him to take my knife and tear it away.

I want his mouth on my peaked nipple, sucking and biting until I can't take it anymore.

Will he make me come too like he made our brother come? I'd felt betrayed that they'd done things without me, but now I feel like I've been brought back into the fold. Like I'm a part of something big—something that the three of us make complete.

"My nipple," I plead between his ravishing kisses. "Touch it. Please."

He growls—actually growls like an animal—and then yanks my bra roughly away from my breast. I cry out in pleasure as his thumb seeks out my nipple. The sensations running through me are intense and incredible, unlike anything I've ever known. When he pinches my nipple between his thumb and middle finger, I feel a jolt of bliss shoot right to my core.

Oh God. I need more.

I need everything.

A scream pierces the air and I pause for a moment, wondering if the sound came from me. A second scream has me wading through the pleasure haze back to reality. It's coming from beyond the fence. Ryder pulls back, lips red and swollen from our kiss. His eyes are manic and filled with ravenous lust. I'm just sure he'll ignore the screams as he eyes my mouth again, but then a gunshot follows.

He's off me and gone in a flash.

CHAPTER TWENTY-SIX

ronan

I T ALL HAPPENS SO FAST.

One minute I'm unzipping Logan's tent for him to set the newly bandaged up Kristen inside, and then the next, she's leaping from his hold to rush out to the group surrounding the fire.

Screaming.

With a gun in hand.

The man she took it from appears to be equally pissed and shocked but backs away from the unstable woman. She wildly swings the weapon around, aiming at anyone she perceives as a threat.

"You all have to run," she croaks out, wild eyes locking on me. "Hurry while you have a chance!"

No one runs. Hell, no one even moves. Except for Logan. He prowls slowly up behind her.

"Th-They'll rape your women and k-kill your kids," she warns. "You're all going to die."

Dad appears in my peripheral, menacing and poised

like he might strike. The tension around the fire is pulled as taut as it will go before snapping.

"Babe," Logan growls.

"NO!" she screams, jerking around to point the gun at him. "NO!

He takes a step forward and she fires the gun.

Pop!

I cry out in horror, waiting for the blood to bloom across his chest. Nothing happens. She missed. Holy shit, she missed. Relief washes over me, but we're not out of the clear yet. A madwoman is still waving a gun around and shooting at people.

Logan darts forward and swings his arm as he moves. He knocks the gun from her shaky grip. I expect him to pick it up, but he keeps going, this time swinging again but at her head.

Crack!

The bones of the back of his hand slam into her cheek. She sways, blinking away her daze, and then he hits her again.

What the fuck?

This time, she goes careening toward the fire. No one does anything. I'm frozen in shock. Dad springs into action first, launching himself toward Kristen. Logan is already charging at her again. This time, his fist rears back.

"I j-just wanted t-to save them," Kristen chants through her tears. "I just w-wanted to save them all."

Dad shoves him away before he can hit the poor

woman again. He hauls her to her feet and then to his side as she sobs uncontrollably. His eyes are flickering wildly as he darts his gaze between Logan, Michael, and Owen, the latter two who sit watching but make no moves to intervene.

"Let me deal with my crazy-ass wife," Logan snarls, chest heaving like he's a charging bull. "I'm not about to let her get away with this shit."

"She's been through a horrific trauma," Dad snaps back. "You will not beat your wife in my goddamn yard."

Logan stalks up to Dad, eyes on Kristen. This isn't going to end well. Both men are big, fearless, and strong.

I frantically look around for my brothers because I feel the need to break this up but can't do it on my own. Rowdy is trotting our way with Mage and Spirit on his heels while Ryder and Raegan burst in through the gate. Thank God.

"What's going on?" Rowdy booms as he enters the circle.

"Hand over my wife," Logan barks at Dad, taking another menacing step toward them. "Now."

Rowdy picks up the discarded gun, which causes the other men in the camp to tense up. CJ and Jace both jolt to their feet, drawing their own weapons. Holy shit, this is escalating fast.

"Stand down," Michael commands, lifting a hand toward CJ and Jace. "You'll only make this worse." Then, to his son, he says, "Logan, that's enough."

Logan ignores him, glowering at Dad. "Wife. Now."

Kristen whimpers and cowers behind my father. Mom enters the fray with Declan on her hip, frowning hard at the situation. Dad grunts Rowdy's name and then nods toward Mom. My brother strides over to Kristen to guide her over to where Mom is standing.

"Take her back to the big house," Dad instructs. "Get the girls out of here too."

Michael slowly makes his way over to where Dad and Logan are facing off like one might approach two dogs who are fighting and doesn't want to get bitten.

Dad is protecting the innocent.

Logan is the predator here.

I'm struck with the sudden realization of how terrifying he is. There's always been something too intense about him. Now I'm understanding it's because this violent man lurks beneath.

He hit his wife.

He almost punched her.

My stomach roils painfully, threatening to rid me of my breakfast. I can't believe I was ever interested in this man. I'd fallen helplessly for his charms. And when I backed off, he was so cold to me. It's because this cruel man is hidden under the façade.

"Let's all just simmer down a minute," Michael urges as he comes to stand beside his son. "Logan just lost his cool. He's sorry. Right, Son?"

Logan transforms before our eyes. The tension bleeds out of him as he falls into a relaxed stance. Fury melts from his features and is replaced with an impassive expression. The abrupt change in him is almost as frightening as the monster he'd unleashed moments before. How can someone turn it on and off so easily?

"I apologize," Logan mutters. "That shouldn't have happened."

Dad scoffs. "You beat your wife in front of my fucking family."

Logan's nostrils flare, the anger peeking back through, but he quickly pushes it away as he opts for a look of chagrin.

"It was inappropriate," Michael agrees. "It won't happen again."

"You're right about that," Dad says, crossing his muscular arms over his chest. "Because you're leaving. All of you."

Silence falls over the camp as everyone digests his words. Despite my earlier feelings about this group, I can't help but feel relief now. I'm thankful Dad is sending them away.

"Now, Reed," Michael starts, but Dad cuts him off with a sharp shake of his head.

"Tomorrow morning. Gone. You can stay the night and get some good rest, but tomorrow, after breakfast, I want you long gone from here." Dad gestures toward the wilderness beyond the fence. "I don't care where as long as we never have to see you again."

Ryder approaches and steps in beside me. "Ro and

I will help them pack up so all that's left for them is to dismantle their tents in the morning."

Logan doesn't look at me and I'm glad. This entire situation has become incredibly awkward.

"What about Stacey?" Michael asks Dad. "You're going to put out a woman who's about to give birth any day now?"

Dad chuckles, but it's not humorous. It's dark and sinister. "You bring a wife beater into my home and you expect me to be sympathetic? You take care of your own…out there." He stabs a finger in the air toward the gate. "I'll take care of mine in here."

And with those final words, Dad has spoken.

Tomorrow, they'll be gone.

I haven't seen Raegan all day and it's eating at me. We never finished our conversation since we were interrupted, which means she'll stay pissed at me until I can make things right.

I *will* make things right.

Raegan is my best friend.

Fighting just isn't something we do.

She said Mom and Dad were the hypocrites, but I'm one too. I was so angry with Ryder for not telling me Dad planned to send him away. And when Raegan was mad I hadn't told her about it, it annoyed me.

I should have told her the second I found out.

She's right. Ryder should have told us together.

I'm sitting on the couch in Ryder's cabin, feeling quite miserable as I watch Chet wave while telling a clearly over-exaggerated story. Ryder and Wild both crack up laughing. I'm not in a laughing mood. In fact, I'm feeling rather depressed.

Ryder is leaving us.

I watch my brother with sick, sad longing. I'm such an idiot. I'd been so desperate for his touch and attention that I never considered he was feeling the pressure to please me. I'm still messed up in the head over him pretending to want me earlier just to distract me.

Does he have to be so damn good-looking?

I can't help but stare at the way his T-shirt stretches over his bulging biceps or the sexy upward curl of his lips on one side. Even his dark eyelashes are mesmerizing—thick and framing his intense eyes.

"I'm going next door," I grunt out. Not that those three even care. "Probably going to sleep over, too."

Ryder's lips tug into a disappointed frown that makes my stomach twist. I hate feeling like the asshole here, but I can't sit and watch him all night. Not after what all went down today. No, I need Raegan. I need my confidant and best friend.

"Don't fuck my sister," Chet calls out unhelpfully as I stuff my feet into my boots. "I'll have to kill you."

A harsh laugh barks out of me. "Don't worry."

Chet tells me to fuck off, clearly misinterpreting my words. I don't think Sadie is some troll. Plus, not only does she lack the proper equipment to interest me, she's also just not Ryder.

As I make it over to the door, I turn once more to get a quick look at Ryder. He's still wearing a pensive expression and he's coiled tight like he might bound over to me to keep me from leaving.

I linger for a long second, giving him the chance if it's what he really wants.

Then, without a word, he turns back to Wild, effectively dismissing me.

Ouch.

Swallowing down the pain that's clawing its way up my throat, I rush out of his cabin and into mine next door. Music is playing on the battery-operated stereo I got one year from Uncle Atticus on my birthday. Sadie is sitting on the floor beside Destiny and is painting her toenails a bright orange color. I flash them a smile before making my way over to the bed where Raegan is sprawled out.

"Hey," I say, voice soft and unsure as I approach.

She bites down on her bottom lip like she wants to keep her expression angry, but a smile peeks through. I let out a swoosh of relieved breath as I lose the boots and climb into bed next to her. Neither of us speaks, but she does snuggle up to me like usual. I wrap my arm around her, pulling her closer. Sadie glances over at us, smirks, and then goes back to her task.

Again, wrong equipment.

Not going to fuck my sister.

I wish I could tell her about earlier. When Ryder got so close we almost kissed again and it might've been with tongue had I let it go on. I want to explain to her that he was playing a game and it hurt so damn much when I realized it. Our brother hurt me and now he'll leave us too, which means the hurt will never go away.

Even though she was upset with me for holding back what Ryder told me, and then my snapping at her, she appears to be over it.

Unusual.

Raegan is a master grudge holder.

"What are you so happy about?" I grumble, playfully tickling her side.

She laughs, her warm breath tickling over me. "That Mya bitch will be gone soon. We should have a party to celebrate."

"I'll bake a cake," Destiny offers.

"I'll bring the booze," Sadie chimes in.

"It'll be a go away party," I offer, "instead of a going away party."

All three girls crack up laughing. When it settles and Destiny and Sadie go back to their quiet conversation, I turn my attention back to Raegan.

"I'm sorry for being a dick earlier." I kiss the top of her head. "You forgive me?"

"Meh," she teases, "I think you could grovel a little more."

I smile up at the ceiling with Raegan glued to my side, listening to the sound of rock music and the giggles come from across the room. Today has gotten significantly better now that I'm here.

Tomorrow, everything will be even better.

Everyone will be gone, and maybe just maybe, we can convince Dad to let Ryder stay.

Then, finally, everything can get back to normal.

CHAPTER TWENTY-SEVEN

ryder

S CREAMING HAUNTS MY DREAMS.

I can't seem to get Kristen's crazed yelling out of my head no matter how much booze I downed last night. All it succeeded in doing was give me a migraine along with my nightmares.

Chet or Wild coughs loudly and then begins their usual snoring.

Sleeping, apparently, isn't in the cards for me.

My mind is a mess. Knowing I have to leave soon to go back to town with Wild's family is absolute torture.

I don't want to go.

I don't want to leave my people…especially Ronan and Raegan.

But maybe Dad is smart about some things. Left to my own devices and I've managed to kiss both my siblings. I've touched them both in places no brother should.

I know what it feels like to have Ronan's hard cock

pressing against my palm or the soft, smooth skin of Raegan's perky breast. And fuck if I don't commit both those memories into my brain forever.

I'll need it to get through the next few months or years.

Alone.

On the hunt for a wife I don't even want.

My thoughts drift back to the pantry. When I'd wanted to distract Ronan from me telling him the truth. He'd accused me of playing him, but I was a hundred percent on board with the idea of capturing his mouth with mine, kissing away all the questions he'd had.

And then what?

Would he have let me touch his cock again?

Could it have gone further?

The thought of someone catching us like that in the pantry, particularly Mom or Dad, has bile creeping up my throat. Nausea hits me in a wave. I pull the pillow tight over my face, hoping to get lost again in the replays of the day.

Which brings my thoughts to Rae.

Holy fuck had that been intense.

She attacked me and cut my damn chin, but then she let me turn the tables. I kissed her like I was starved for her taste. My dick ground against her, aching for relief. The best part was, I pinched her hard nipple and would have found a way to get it into my mouth had Kristen not screamed.

Again.

As though that memory is on repeat, I hear it again. Far away. Repeated several times.

Chet has a coughing fit. And then, so does Wild.

What the hell?

I jerk my pillow off my face and am met with the smell of smoke wafting through the air. At first I think it's a nightmare come to life, but then I quickly realize it's not a dream.

"Wake up!" I yell, my voice croaking with sleep. "Wild, there's smoke!"

Wild curses and then shoves his foot into Chet's side. "Dude, wake up. Fire."

Chet scrambles up quickly but then has a coughing fit. While he tries to catch his breath, I shove on my boots and burst out of the cabin. Thick smoke covers everything around me, limiting visibility to barely an arm's length in front of me.

What the hell happened?

Through the orange hazy smoke, I realize the fire is coming from the big house. As I race toward it, I discover nearly half of the home is on fire.

"Mom!" I yell into the house, shying away from the immense heat of it. "Fuck, Dad!"

Nothing.

And then I hear it.

The screams I'd heard before. Not my dreams. Real life.

Dawson.

He's not even a year old. If something happened to

Mom and Dad, he'd never be able to get out on his own.
Cursing at what I have to do, I rush around to a part
of the house that's not quickly burning to the ground.
With my elbow, I bash in the glass and then jerk the
window up so I can crawl through it. A burst of heat
surges out the window, causing me to groan.

This is going to suck so bad.

Dawson's howl of terror has me hoisting myself
through the window without further thought. The
smoke is thicker inside and the heat is fucking unbear-
able. I'm instantly drenched in sweat and overcome with
a coughing fit that makes me dizzy. Blindly, I stumble through the house in an effort to steer clear of the
kitchen and dining room area that seem to be where
the fire started.

I make it to Declan and Kota's room first. When I
burst inside, I'm happy to see both their beds are empty.
Maybe Dad grabbed them and got them out of here
already. Next, I fling open the door to Destiny and
Raegan's room that's our current infirmary. Kristen is
gone, of course, but now, so is Stacey. The only one remaining is Carter.

"Carter, man, we have to get you out of here," I
boom, rushing over to him. "What the fuck?"

A knife is planted deep in the center of his chest.

He's dead.

Someone stabbed him.

Panic swells up inside of me and I race down to my
parents' room. Their bedroom is closer to the living

room that's quickly being overtaken by the inferno, so when I touch their doorknob, it burns the hell out of my palm.

With several hard kicks, I knock the door in and it flings out of my way.

"Mom! Dawson!"

My baby brother wails from the other side of the bed. The bed that's empty. Where the hell are my parents? I practically hurdle myself over the bed in an effort to find my brother. What I discover has me freezing in terror.

"Mom?"

She's covered in blood and has Dawson in her tight grip. Her eyes are wide and her lips are curled into a vicious sneer. When I go to reach for my brother, she swipes at me with a knife, tearing through the fabric of my T-shirt. A fucking knife!

"Mom! Stop!"

"You can't take my baby!" she screams at me. "You can't take my baby!"

This time, I anticipate the knife swipe and grab hold of her arm. Easily, I wrench it away from her and throw it out of her reach. Then, I scoop them both up together.

Dawson's screaming is interrupted by a coughing fit that has him gagging. And all the blood that's on Mom appears to be hers based on the moans of pain that escape her as I move.

I have to get them out of here.

Stepping into the doorway, I feel the intense heat of

the flames inching closer. Thankfully, I can head back the way I came from without running into any fires. I run as fast as my legs will carry me while holding two people, and eventually make it back to the window at the end of the hall.

"Here!" a deep, familiar voice barks. "Hand her to me."

I feed Mom and Dawson through the window into the arms of…Rowdy. As soon as I see my older brother's familiar face, I choke out a relieved sob. He takes over the physically demanding task of getting Mom and Dawson away from the house that's perishing quicker than ever.

As soon as I'm out of the house, I quickly scan the smoky yard, looking for the others. I need to find Dad and Kota and Declan. I scramble all over the place, searching by the campfire and then where the tents were erected.

Nothing.

The tents are gone and so are the people.

Wild and Chet show up to where Rowdy is kneeling to look at Mom's wounds. Wild crouches to pick up Dawson. Both guys are wide-eyed and wearing matching bewildered expressions.

"We have to find Dad and the other kids," I tell them, voice nearly gone from all the smoke. "I'm going to grab Ronan and Raegan to help. Meet me by the gate."

"I got this," Rowdy assures me. "Find our family."

I take off in a sprint back toward the cabins, choking

on the thick clouds of pungent smoke. Finally, I reach Ronan's cabin and burst through the door.

"Wake up," I holler at them. "Everything's on fire, Mom's been stabbed, Carter's dead, and half our family is missing!"

Nothing.

A poisonous seed of dread takes root in the pit of my stomach.

"Raegan! Destiny! Sadie!"

Still nothing.

If I find my sisters and brothers stabbed like Carter, I'll fucking die.

I scramble over to Ronan's solar-powered lamp and twist the knob. Yellow light illuminates the space. No dead bodies. Thank fuck.

But that means they're missing too.

Based on the way the blankets have been dragged off the bed, shoes scattered, and furniture sitting crooked, I'd say there was a struggle. I notice Ronan's glasses sitting on the wood floor, smashed to pieces, as if someone crushed them under their heavy boot. Panic seizes my chest. I yank open his side table drawer to find his three extra pairs sitting neatly and untouched.

He wouldn't willingly leave his glasses behind.

Oh God.

"Wild sent me—" Chet starts and then says, "Where the fuck is Sadie?"

"My siblings are gone too," I hiss out. "Something bad has happened. Something really bad."

"Maybe they went to get fresh air," Chet suggests, fighting another cough. "Like we should be doing."

I shake my head in vehemence. "No. Carter was stabbed. Mom was attacked. Someone hurt them."

My first thought is the rapists who attacked Kristen. They must've come back. But there were only two of them supposedly. I also doubt they'd take the time to dismantle tents.

They wouldn't do that because they don't exist.

Holy fucking shit.

It was *them*.

The trespassers.

They were playing us all along.

I bolt out the door, shoving past Chet, and race toward the gate that stands wide open. Beyond the gate, there's nothing to see except more smoky woods. The visibility is worse away from the light of the fire. I'm cursing myself for having not grabbed a flashlight.

"Wild's truck is gone," Chet exclaims, doubled over as he sucks in air. "He parked it right there."

It's then that I see the form of a body. I can't breathe as I make my way over to it. Dark, messy hair shields the woman's face from me.

No.

Please, God, no.

Crouching, I recognize the woman. Thankfully, it's not Raegan. It's Carter's mom, Wendy. She's littered with bloody wounds that also look to have come from a knife, though I don't see one anywhere.

Who the hell would do this?

"Someone stabbed her to death?" Chet cries out in horror. "What kind of redneck freaks are you people? Where the hell is my goddamn sister?"

Ignoring him, I sprint over to another form. This time, it's a bald older man. Another one from the trespasser's group named Gary. Beside him are his wife, son, daughter-in-law, and three grandchildren, including their six-month-old.

All slaughtered like pigs.

Bloody and viciously stabbed.

I'm going to be sick.

I lose count of the deaths when I stumble upon a couple more bodies. Hellie and her young son, Nicky.

All dead. All stabbed and dragged out here to rot.

The outlook for finding my siblings and father isn't looking good.

That's eleven corpses.

Where are Logan and the rest of the trespassers?

And *my* people.

Where the hell are *my* people?

Where're Ronan and Raegan and Destiny? What about Dad and Kota and Declan? Chet's sister, Sadie?

A grunting sound from up the road draws my attention. I prowl toward the sound, fear winding around my throat like a vise. A figure lies in the road, groaning and squirming. As I approach, I recognize it.

"Dad!"

He's barely distinguishable on his face. Someone

beat the fuck out of him. His eyes are swollen shut and his lips are twice their normal size. Blood is splattered all over him. I recognize his hair and beard, though.

They hurt my mom and dad.

Furious tears burn at my eyes, but I refuse to let them fall. I drop to the ground beside Dad to assess his injuries. His arms are bound behind him as are his feet. It's as though someone dragged him out of bed because he's wearing just a black pair of boxers. His entire body is bloody. It's then I notice the rope around his neck.

What the fuck?

His hissed breaths are coming out softer and less frequent. I move his beard out of the way and start tugging at the rope that's suffocating him. This time, the tears do fall, wetting my sooty cheeks. My fingers feel too clumsy as I work to untie the rope. As I'm pulling the long end through one of the loops to loosen it, I notice it's been cut.

Had they tied my father to the back of Wild's truck and dragged him?

Until someone had pity on him and cut the rope?

My heart stutters to a stop.

Raegan.

She never leaves without her knife.

"It's okay, Dad. I've got you. Mom's alive. So is the baby."

He rasps out a groan and then starts coughing like crazy. I'm stunned stupid. I don't know what to do or where to go. My family is gone and the other half is near dead.

A sharp pain lances through my chest as my new reality sinks in.

My family was taken.

They took them.

They *fucking* took them.

But I will find my people.

I'll raze the entire goddamn state of Alaska to the ground just to get them back if I have to.

And I *will* get them back.

Even if I die trying.

To be continued…

I hope you enjoyed this book!
Dying to continue their story?
Read *The Unruly* next!
authorkwebster.com/product/the-unruly

Want to read a steamy a free Daddy Reed short story?
Check it out here: https://dl.bookfunnel.com/6t7xcdpupc

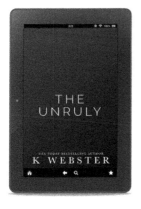

MORE TABOO ROMANCE IS COMING...

Thank you for reading!

Our love is untamed.
And we are the unruly.

THE UNRULY

ABOUT THE AUTHOR

K Webster is a *USA Today* Bestselling author. Her titles have claimed many bestseller tags in numerous categories, are translated in multiple languages, and have been adapted into audiobooks. She lives in "Tornado Alley" with her husband, two children, and her baby dog named Blue. When she's not writing, she's reading, drinking copious amounts of coffee, and researching aliens.

To see the full list of K Webster's books, visit authorkwebster.com/all-books.

JOIN MY NEWSLETTER
at authorkwebster.com/newsletter

JOIN MY PRIVATE GROUP
at www.facebook.com/groups/krazyforkwebstersbooks

Follow K Webster here!

Facebook: www.facebook.com/authorkwebster

Readers Group:
www.facebook.com/groups/krazyforkwebstersbooks

Patreon: patreon.com/authorkwebster

Twitter: twitter.com/KristiWebster

Goodreads:
www.goodreads.com/author/show/7741564.K_Webster

Instagram: www.instagram.com/authorkwebster

BookBub: www.bookbub.com/authors/k-webster

Wattpad: www.wattpad.com/user/kwebster-wildromance

TikTok: www.tiktok.com/@authorkwebster

Pinterest: www.pinterest.com/kwebsterwildromance

LinkedIn: www.linkedin.com/in/k-webster-396b7021

Milton Keynes UK
Ingram Content Group UK Ltd.
UKHW020910220424
441551UK00017B/1101